INTUITION

Cover Design and Interior Format

INTUITION

Jenni Bradley

For Kim Hanson, one of my biggest cheerleaders. Without you this book would never have been written. Thank you for encouraging and demanding more and more from me. Without your gentle nudges, I would have serious writer's block!

CHAPTER 1

I SAT IN MY CAR, FREEZING my ass off outside of some dive bar and waiting for my mark. I had hung around for three worthless hours, waiting for the dumb schmuck to walk out of the bar with his flavor of the month. Thankfully, my semi-warm coffee was half-full and kept a tiny part of my misery at bay. I blew a heavy lung-filled breath out, watching the condensation form a smoky cloud as though I were Puff the Magic Dragon. This fall night felt more like the dead of winter. I yearned to start my car but didn't want to look like a weirdo sitting in an idling car. It would be a dead giveaway that I was watching for something or someone. *Who knew if this guy had friends who would tip him off?* People, with things to hide, were plumb paranoid. At least, in my line of work they were. The unpredictable nature of my job had instilled a healthy dose of precaution, on my part.

My mother had wanted me to find a respectable husband and take care of our two children while tending to our home. She had expected my life to consist of PTA meetings and shuttling our kiddos to every extra-curricular activity known to man. I didn't have an ounce of Martha Stewart in my genes. Of course, if I had, I wouldn't be sitting in my car, spying on a sleazy, cheating husband. Or so the wife who hired me had wanted me to find out. I hate to admit it, but a wife's intuition is rarely wrong.

In reality, I had become a private investigator. Which had become a sore subject for my mother. I graduated from Purdue University with a degree in business. I had worked in a multitude of settings, all of which were minimum paying jobs. Not one of them had come close to paying the bills. A clause should be mandatory on all college applications: although you obtain your degree, it by no means guarantees you a well-paying career after graduation.

I was out looking for a second job when I saw an ad in the paper for a receptionist for a small PI firm, Donovan Investigations. I immediately applied for the position, not all that enthused about it. Greta, the lady I would be replacing, was retiring and it paid more than my current clothing store position did. I jumped at the offer and haven't looked back since.

I hired in as the new receptionist. I profusely begged the sexiest boss I had ever had the pleasure of working under––er, I mean for––to let me fill the temporary private investigator position. I had a short period of time to prove myself worthy of the role before he hired someone permanent and I went back to filing. Which, I am happy to report, that my filing skills were up to par. Those first months were tough. I worked around the clock, obtaining the hours for the PI license on top of my secretarial duties. With hard work and many sleepless nights, I finally obtained my license. On the downside, I was still stuck in my administrative duties until I found a suitable replacement.

Thus far, every client I had taken on had been happy with my results. Well, happy was a relative term. When they found out that their spouse was cheating, they were not one bit jovial. I took on these cases because following spouses around and taking pictures was not hard. More time-consuming than anything, with a hell of a lot of patience thrown in. I sucked at the whole patience thing. It wasn't my forte, but I was working on that.

I snatched my e-cigarette from the cup holder, pushed the button, and sucked in the nicotine. This was my only chance at quitting the real thing. I loved to smoke but I needed a healthier option. This way, I got my nicotine fix without the other nasty little chemicals that saturated my lungs. After a couple of puffs, I put the e-cig down, feeling marginally better.

Before my mark was due to arrive, I had sat in the run-down bar, scoping the place out. I made sure to locate all of the potential exits. The one in the back was for employees only. The front was his only option. Plus, I needed visual confirmation that it was actually the guy and not his doppelganger. Once the douchebag strolled in and saddled up to the bar, I finished my O'Doul's in a glass and headed out to my car and waited. I was jonesing to pick up my tablet and read one of my sizzling romances but the second I did, I would miss my chance. Not to mention that the light from the screen would light up the car like high beams to oncoming traffic on a bleak country. It's difficult to adjust your eyesight and take useful pictures when your eyes keep the outline of the bright tablet haloed around your vision. Those precious seconds could make or break the case.

The quicker I gathered the incriminating evidence, the quicker I closed the case, and received the rest of the money. Retainers don't pay all the bills and I liked my smut. I tried to budget my book purchases but it was a hopelessly lost cause. I lived pretty frugally as it was and reading was my only guilty pleasure at the moment. Not like my love life was anything to speak of right now. I guess you could say I was going through a dry spell at the moment. More like two years of strictly vibrator action. I should invest in Duracell stock. The Energizer Bunny runs out of steam with extended use. Which should be another mandatory clause boldly printed on the back of the battery package.

I took another hit off my e-cig, blew out the mist, and turned my wrist over to glance at my watch. At this rate, the bar would close before he emerged. Fuck, I didn't have all night. Michael, my mark, was a good-looking guy. He had an athletic build, with a full head of hair. He carried a confidence that made the ladies flock to his side. I was completely unaffected seeing as he was married. Some women didn't seem to be bothered by that little detail. Then again, when he came into the bar, my eyes were drawn to his ring finger and found it bare. Upon closer inspection, you could identify the tiny imprint that the ring had left behind. A bare ring finger was enough for most women to not need any further confirmation of a guy's marital status. A simple lie from his lips would further confirm his bachelorhood.

The thing that stuck in my craw with this guy was that he seemed to have it all. His wife was beautiful. She kept herself well-manicured. When she had visited me at the office, her nails were done, her makeup was lightly applied, and her hair perfectly styled. How she had managed to appear flawless when she had a one-year-old kid amazed the hell out of me. If I were in the same position, I would be wearing yoga pants, a stained shirt, and my hair would be thrown haphazardly into a ponytail. My closet would be filled with comfy wool-lined Crocs. Makeup would totally be an afterthought and way too much trouble than it was worth.

The light from inside the bar spilled out in to the dark night, catching my attention. I carefully grabbed my camera. The settings had already been put on the desired shutter speed. I zoomed in on the smiling Glen as he wrapped his arms around a thin brunette with too much hairspray and snapped about fifty pictures as he glided them to his car. He opened the passenger door for her and before she climbed in, he pulled her against his body and slammed his mouth over hers. My shutter continued its clicking as I spied on them through the lens. I started my car as soon as he slid into the driver seat. I waited until he pulled out of the parking lot before I followed.

It was a piece of cake to follow them to the hotel a couple of blocks down. The brunette had fully engaged his attention. He would have a hard time picking up a tail when his passenger was giving his neck a tongue bath. *So gross!* I pulled in as he walked through the automatic doors of the hotel chain. I found a parking spot that gave me optimal advantage for my camera. I snapped him exiting the hotel, as well as the two of them reentering. I snapped the cover over the lens and stowed my camera back in its protective compartment. I spent a ton of cash purchasing this camera. It was my bread and butter, providing me the quality I needed, and it had already paid for itself.

I had enough evidence to prove to his wife that he was, in fact, cheating on her. There was no need for me to wait for them to check out. I plugged in my phone and scrolled through my artists until I found Kid Rock. I loved his gravelly and humbled voice. I cranked up the volume as I headed back to the office to download the SIM card. He was one of my favorite artists. He'd make you cry, shout profanities, and nod your head to the classic rock beat. He had a song for every emotional outlet.

I pulled up to the brownstone that housed our offices, ogling the nostalgic building. Every time my eyes soaked in the building, my body felt a sense of peace and belonging. It wasn't any one particular thing that generated this feeling. I couldn't pinpoint the origin. If I was honest with myself, I didn't care to know the hows and the whys. The only thing that mattered was that it did. I belonged here, working alongside Nash as well as the other PIs. If I could fuck the crankiness out of Nash, my life would be complete. He growled at me constantly, never at Ryker or Hawke, the other two PIs. Then again, they have some kind of brotherhood relationship. I'm not sure how they knew one another. I didn't question the dynamics. It's not any of my business, even though the questions sat heavily in my chest as though I had a bad case of heartburn. They had made it abundantly clear the day I was hired that they were not open to sharing intimate details of their lives.

I climbed the stairs two at a time, excited to put this case to bed. I hated to have to give her the bad news but it was what I was paid to do. She would be better without him. The alimony alone would set her up for the rest of her life. She wouldn't have to work and could raise her daughter how she wanted. It was a win–win, in my book. After some time passed, she would be able see reason and be glad that she had found out the truth. At least that's what I had hoped. There was nothing worse to me than living a lie.

I rushed passed Nash's office, not daring to peek in. I knew he was there because his truck was parked in his usual spot.

"Briggs, get your ass in my office," he barked out.

Damn. I was so close. He had an uncanny knack of knowing exactly where I was. No matter how unsettling it may be, I relished in its sweet comfort. I about-faced and headed straight through his office door. I plopped into the oversized chair that sat opposite of his masculine oak desk. I mentally sighed at his dark, brooding sexiness. I tried like hell to remain as impassive as I could. Even though his mere presence flooded my system as rapidly as the water surged over the falls of Niagara.

"What's up, boss man?" I oozed saccharinely.

"Why are you back at the office this late?" His voice deepened another notch.

I barely managed to stop my eyes from rolling. "I got the final proof for one of my cases. I wanted to get them downloaded before tomorrow. This way I could call Brenda first thing in the morning and get it closed out."

He gentled his tone. "It could have waited until morning."

I smiled at his softer side. "I didn't want to wait. Now I can sleep with a clear conscience, knowing that the pictures are safely stored on my hard drive."

"All right then. I won't keep you."

I swiftly pulled myself from the comfortable chair and hightailed it to my office before I lost myself in his steel-gray eyes. Knowing my luck, I probably left a wet spot on the chair. God, that man was put on this earth solely to please a woman—mainly this woman. My vagina screamed all sorts of nasty words at me for leaving his office. I sat at my desk and ran my hands along my face, utterly sexually frustrated. I lay my head on the desk and banged it against the hard wood, trying to dispel my growing attraction for my boss.

"Are you sure you're okay?"

I lifted my head at the swift pace of a snail. *Could my humiliation become any worse?* I caught the slight twitch of his lips with my eyes as I finally made contact with his chiseled facial features. His lips begged to be kissed. They were full and arousing. I bet they were as soft as they appeared. With the right amount of pressure those lips could have you skyrocketing into the next atmosphere.

I counted to three as I let out a breath, trying to regulate my rapid heartbeat. "Yeah. It's been a long day. Nothing a bed can't cure." My cheeks instantly heated as my remark registered.

He let out a husky chuckle that shot straight to my nether regions. My lids opened wider and my mouth went slack.

"Finish up and go warm up your bed." His comment went bedroom husky and his jaw muscles clenched.

I stared after his retreating back. He had turned and went back to his office as silently as he had entered mine.

Jesus, what the hell was wrong with me? I had worked alongside him for almost a year now. Today was no different from the last three hundred and some. I needed to get laid. If I didn't, I feared for Nash's safety. There was no telling when my self-control would snap and I would physically jump on him, demanding him to ease the ache. He had never insinuated that our relationship was anything more than boss and employee.

It's not that I was ugly. If I had to put myself in a particular category, I'd say that I was the girl next-door type with a naturally athletic build. Not that I did any exercise to keep it that way. I had an ample bust size, straight white teeth—despite many years of smoking—and artic-blue eyes. I kept my chestnut hair a little past my shoulders, with blonde highlights woven throughout. I could get a man if I wanted but I had focused most of my time and energy in proving myself to Nash that I wanted this position. It hadn't left enough time to form a meaningful relationship with the opposite sex. Cutting aside the bullshit, I only wanted one man and he remained less than fifty feet from me but oceans apart emotionally.

I huffed out another frustrated breath while I inserted the SIM card with more force than necessary. *Shit!* Reining in my frustration took as long as it did to download the pictures. I created a new folder and labeled it Glen. Before I took out the SIM, I made sure to click on every picture to ensure that the quality was pristine. I deleted the ones that weren't. I could not pass off a bad picture. The wife might refute the evidence if they were not perfect. If I had to do another stakeout, I would. Thankfully, these pictures depicted Glen and his lover exceptionally well. There was no denying that it was her husband. I powered down the computer and packed away the equipment. I stowed my camera back in the safe that I kept in my office. I would no longer need it tonight.

I shut the light off and closed my office door. "Night, Nash. See you in the morning," I called out, not bothering to stop. There was no need to torture myself any further.

"Night, Skye."

My body shivered as the huskiness of his voice caressed every inch of my body. When he used my last name, I knew he was in a serious mood. When he used my first name, it rolled off his tongue intimately. Too bad he didn't use it very often. I counted my lucky stars that the drive home was short. I was running on empty. My eyeballs felt as though they were fighting a sandstorm at the moment. I strolled into my darkened home and headed straight for bed. There was no need for lights. I had memorized the layout years ago. I kept a pretty tidy house simply because I was never in it. I peeled my clothes off and dove under the covers. The great thing about living alone was that I could walk around naked all I wanted and I most certainly did.

CHAPTER 2

WHY DID THE SUN HAVE to be so damn bright? I cracked open my swollen eyelids, wishing that I could continue to hibernate under the covers for the rest of the day. Unfortunately, the bills don't pay themselves and as far as I know, I hadn't woken up rich. That would have been a pleasant surprise. I pulled back the beckoning comforter and slid clumsily out of bed. I was definitely not a morning person. It took me at least five strong cups of coffee before I could think properly. Some days I threw the creamer right in the glass bowl and drank from the pot.

I stumbled around my place until the caffeine hit my system. After I had two cups of coffee and the nicotine from my e-cig, I was coherent enough to drive to the office. I had to have my wits about me when I was there. Working in a male-dominated atmosphere demanded that I be at the top of my game at all times.

Ryker and Hawke were ex-military and just as badass as the day they were honorably discharged from the Delta Force. That's all I basically gathered from the minimal information I had on them. I didn't even know whether they had first names or not. They were built like brick houses, with intimidation written all over them. They didn't need last names. They were that cool. Nash was a whole different specimen. He was bigger than Ryker and Hawke and meaner. His muscles had muscles but they weren't the veiny muscles that the extreme bodybuilders get. His were sleek and sexy. In my fantasies, I'd run my fingers along the valleys and ridges that made up his body. My imagination ran wild with scenes of him and me in the bedroom. Nash was the ultimate Alpha male and his background was even more convoluted than Ryker and Hawke's.

I shook my head, clearing the images of Nash naked, and neutralized my face before I headed into the office. With my game face on and a coffee in my hand, I stormed up the steps. I called out a hello to whoever was listening. A bunch of mumbles rang out. I grinned to myself, enjoying the nominal banter. They were coming around. It wouldn't be long and I would have them muttering two-word sentences.

I glanced at the clock. I had an hour to get everything together for my meeting with Mrs. McGonnel. I powered on the computer and waited for it to load. I put in the SIM card and printed out the whole file. I linked my hands together behind my head and leaned back in the chair while propping my feet up on the desk. I closed my eyes and listened to the steady drum of the printer.

"That's the poster image of hard work, right there."

My body jerked at the sound of Nash's baritone voice. Which, in turn, caused the backrest to tilt farther. My arms splayed out to my sides, trying to right myself. My feet went straight into the air and I fell out of the chair. The momentum carried my ass over my head and into an awkward backward roll that fell short of completion. *Oh, lordy!* I was stuck with my ass sticking in the air. I hope my pants stayed in place and I didn't flash him my crack. *That would be beyond humiliating.*

The deep chuckle had me popping back into my current predicament.

"Uh, can I get a little help or are you going to continue to stand there and ogle my backside?" My voice was mumbled due to my mouth being smashed into my cleavage.

"I don't know. I kind of like you in this position. Completely at my mercy." All traces of humor were now replaced with a commanding huskiness.

I squeezed my eyes shut. Now was not the time to let my hormones out of their cage. "Please, help me up. This isn't very comfortable."

"Hmm. You did say please."

I could hear the mischievousness in his voice.

He righted the chair and moved it to the side in one swift motion. He placed his thighs against my lower back and ass. My ass aligned perfectly with his hips. *Fuck.* My hormones busted out of their pen and heated my blood with their cries for release.

"Wrap your legs around my waist and raise your arms toward me," he commanded gruffly.

I couldn't breathe as it was but when he bent between my legs, grabbed my wrists, and pulled me up against his firm chest––the rest of the oxygen in my body promptly left. I gawked at him, on the verge of a full-blown fantasy. Involuntarily, my thighs tightened around him. I wiggled, needing the friction of his body to ease the intense ache.

"Skye?" he murmured throatily.

"Hmm," I purred.

"Briggs?" he snapped authoritatively.

I blinked my eyes and snapped to attention. "Oh, ah––right."

One-syllable words were all I could form at the moment. I was starting to sound like the guys. Heat rose to my cheeks. My humiliation level elevated to the point that I thought I'd puke. I immediately unwrapped my legs from around him and shakily put them back on the floor. I took a giant step back, with my eyes downcast.

"Mrs. McGonnel is in the conference room," he informed me casually, as though I hadn't just tried to dry-hump him.

I nodded my head and walked over to the printer, not even daring myself to glance in his direction. I had maxed out my limit of embarrassing moments today. When I finally pumped up the courage to look at him, he had already disappeared. With every step I took toward the conference room, I mentally slapped myself. I was sure that little episode would put me well within range of sexual harassment.

"I know you found the proof that I needed," she rapidly fired as soon as I opened the door.

"Mrs. McGonnel, I am not going to sugarcoat this. Everything I found is detailed in this file, including photographs. You can choose to go through the file that I compiled or you can leave it unopened on the table and walk out of here," I said as plainly as I could.

I pulled out the chair next to her. I swiveled around to face her. I took in her drab appearance. Gone was the confident woman who visited my office a week ago. Her hair was ratty and unwashed. The tracksuit she wore hung loose around her already petite frame. I grabbed her hands and held onto them firmly. I wanted to infuse some of my energy into her.

"Mrs. McGonnel, I'm not sure what I would do if I found out my husband was cheating on me. What I do know is that you have a very loving and dependent little one who is going to need your strength. This is not the end but merely a beginning."

She slowly picked her head up from her chest. Her eyes were bright with unshed tears. "A beginning? How can you say that?" She sniffed.

"A new start to figure out what you want out of life. It's your time to forge your own path. You have the ability to raise your kiddo the way that you want to. There is no one to answer to or convince that your way of raising your child is the best way. Most importantly, you no longer have to worry about what Michael is doing, where he is going, and with whom he is spending his time. He is no longer a part of the equation. He made his choice and it has nothing to do with you. It was his decision to ruin the best thing in the world: a loving wife, beautiful baby, and a home."

Of course, I couldn't be certain of that but I wanted her walking out of here with her chin held high. I wanted to give her the get-out-of-marriage card with guilt free strings. She wouldn't have to compromise because of their kid.

A slow smile emerged on her puffy face. "You are right. Thank you, Miss Briggs. I know exactly what I am going to do. Can I have this file for my lawyer?"

"Absolutely. You are welcome to the file."

I stood with her. She embraced me in a tight hug. I squeezed back.

"Thank you, again."

I nodded and watched her walk through the conference doors with her head held high and rocking the baggy tracksuit. I sank back into the leather chair. I raised my fingers to my temples and gently rubbed the throbbing area. Cheating cases wore me out. I never liked confirming the wife's suspicions. I maintained a sliver of hope that one day the spouse would defy the repetitive outcome. Witnessing a marriage dissolve never gave me the accolades of a job well done.

Deft fingers set three little pain relievers and a glass of water in front of me. I greedily snatched them up and popped them into my mouth. I mumbled my thanks before I chased them with the iced-cold water.

I angled my body toward Nash. "Got a case for me?"

He slid the file across the table, never saying a word.

With shaky hands, I tentatively opened the file. I never knew what kind of information those files contained. It could be more surveillance on a spouse, for all I knew. Nash was serious most of the time, so it was hard to guess what case he would send my way. Usually, they were the ones that Ryker and Hawke didn't have time for. I was low man on the totempole so it didn't bother me. I looked at it as putting in my time. I had to earn my stripes.

Normally, I'd skim through the pages because, quite honestly, reading through the details bored me to death. It was like reading the last page of the book to find out what happened before I read through the second chapter. I sat, dumbfounded, as I read through every page. I must have sat there for a half an hour before I looked up at Nash. The same neutral expression was on his chiseled face.

"Are you shitting me? Am I being punked?" I squirmed enthusiastically.

There was no way in hell he would give me something like this.

His eyes sparkled with silent laughter. "No to both of your questions. I think you are ready to get your feet wet. You've proved yourself." He pushed his chair away from the table. "Take the rest of the day to get familiar with the case. I'll be in if you have any questions. All of the information you need is in the file."

I nodded, unsure, of what would come out of my mouth if I spoke. I stared at the manila folder long enough for my eyes to water. *Holy shit! Nash trusted me with a missing person's case.* I picked up the file, careful not to lose any of the papers tucked inside, and walked back to my office in a state of disbelief.

I slumped into my chair. This was exciting and yet beyond my comfort zone. *Hello! I've been following around two-bit losers and dealing with crazy retail people.* What the heck did I know about solving a missing person's case? *If the local police couldn't solve it, how the hell did Nash think that I would?* I didn't have a clue or the credentials to accomplish this. *Where did I even begin?*

"First thing first, study the case. Know it like the back of your hand."

I jumped, startled that Nash stood confidently in the doorway. I stared at him completely flabbergasted. "How do you do that?"

"Do what?"

"Sneak up on me and know what I'm thinking?" I shook my head.

"You are an open book. Every emotion you feel is broadcasted all over your face. You can do this. Read the file and see if you pick up anything. Don't second-guess yourself. Come to me with anything. I'll be right here if you need me." With that, he silently exited.

Guess I should start at the beginning. I shoved the files into my briefcase and took an early quit. I earned it.

CHAPTER 3

GRAY, A SIXTEEN-YEAR-OLD, WENT MISSING about two years ago. She had good grades and went to church every Sunday with her mother. The file stated that she had been a focused student and seemed to get along with everyone at her local high school. She was five feet, seven inches tall, with pin-straight shoulder-length hair. Her hazel eyes were vivid, with the green spiraling through the brown. On the day that she went missing, her mother had taken her home from school early when she had felt ill. According the mother's statement, she had left her at home and returned back to school. When she had arrived home later on that day, her daughter was no longer there. She immediately called the police but the missing person's case would not be filed for another twenty-four hours.

My stomach felt queasy with the knowledge that this young woman had not been found. The possibilities of what could have happened rolled in nauseating waves. *What must her poor parents be going through?* Determination set in my bones. Whatever it took, I would find out what happened and bring closure to her family. I hoped to find her alive, but after this length of time, the possibility was practically zero.

The urge to call my mother nearly bowled me over. Her constant nagging over my lackluster life was how the majority of our fights began. That didn't mean I didn't love her. Did she get on my nerves? Yes, but at the moment, I needed to hear her voice.

"Skye, how are you, baby?"

Mom had picked up on the first ring.

"I'm good, Mom. What are you and Dad doing today?" I asked sincerely.

"I'm trying to get your dad to take an art class with wine."

"No way in hell. I'm not going somewhere, drinking wine and painting something cheesy. I'm going to sit in my underwear and watch the game, drinking beer like a real man," he hollered in the background.

"You see what I live with! He needs to get out of the house. Ever since he retired, he has been a bump on a log. No fun whatsoever."

Laughter bubbled up and poured out. "Maybe he would go with you if you were going to hot yoga."

"What's that, dear?"

I laughed harder. "Look it up online. Have fun trying to get him to go."

"I will later. Tell me about you. How's work? Have you found a nice boy yet?"

I groaned inwardly. "It's going well. Nash gave me a new case to work on. I'm really excited about it. All right Mom, I have to get going. Let me know how your painting party goes. Love you."

"Love you too, dear."

I hung up feeling emotionally better. Annoyance aside, I loved them, and on occasion they were slightly comical.

The theme for *Mission Impossible* chimed as my ringtone for Nash.

"What's up, boss?"

"Meet me in the office parking lot in fifteen."

He had hung up before I could ask why. I'd rather be meeting him at his place but the parking lot would do.

I arrived in the parking lot with five minutes to spare and of course Nash was leaning against the brick with his thumbs hooked in the front pockets. James Dean made that pose sexy. Nash made it downright X-rated. He pushed off the wall and strode toward his car, motioning for me to get in.

Oh, a secret tryst; yes, please. I walked on shaky legs toward his truck. My sweaty hand slid right off the door handle as I tried to open it. The momentum knocked me off balance. I quickly recovered, wiped my palms on the thighs of my jeans, and tried it again. The door opened and I climbed up. His chuckles reverberated through my already heated skin.

"You just get the car waxed?" I asked, trying to hide my faux pas.

"Nope."

Wonderful. I turned into a complete jackass when I was in his presence.

"Where are you taking me?"

"The range to practice your shot."

My eyes widened with giddiness. "Seriously?"

He nodded, effectively shutting down any

further conversation. Shortly after Nash had hired me, I had filled out the paperwork for my carry-conceal. I was now legal to carry a firearm. That didn't mean that I always did. I guess, in our line of work, I should start. All the guys did. Their bodies were a walking advertisement for a weapon factory. I shivered at the thought of undressing and finding Nash's secret hiding spots.

I followed nervously through the doors of the range. The thought of Nash watching me made my stomach flip anxiously. I rolled my eyes toward the fluorescent bulbs, praying that I wouldn't do anything stupid, like shoot a finger off. We signed the paperwork and grabbed the items we needed. Our lanes were right next to each other. He placed a box of bullets and a Walther PK380 on the ledge.

"Check the clip and the chamber to make sure that there are no live rounds."

I did as I was told with shaky fingers. I showed him the empty clip and chamber.

"Make sure the safety is on and go ahead and load your clip. Once the clip is loaded, I want you to rack the slide, and then get into your firing stance."

I followed his instructions to a T. I stood with my legs shoulder width apart and my knees slightly bent. I reached out with my arms locked in front. My eyes focused through the sight, locking onto the paper target.

"Once you're locked on your target, put your finger on the trigger. Breathe in for a count of three and then pull the trigger on your exhale. Make sure you exhale through the shot."

My heart rate increased dramatically as adrenaline poured into my bloodstream. I felt somewhat light-headed but managed to follow through. On three, I pulled the trigger. The hot shell flew across my line of vision and bounced off the wall of the lane, making a pinging sound as it landed on the concrete floor. The smell of sulfur made my nose twitch. I set the gun down and looked over my shoulder.

"Well done. Let's keep going." He stepped over to his lane.

I got into position and fired again. When the target was full of holes, I replaced it with another. I was on my last rounds. I racked the slide with my last full clip in place when I felt a pinch. I dropped the gun with a whimper. I could see some of my skin trapped in the slide. I bit down hard on my lower lip to hold back the tears. I peeked at the cut skin between my thumb and pointer finger. *Shit!* The tender flesh throbbed and burned. I hadn't bled that much most of it had pooled under the remaining skin.

"How bad is it?"

I jumped at the sound of Nash's alarmed voice.

"Not too bad. Hurts worse than it looks." Surprisingly, my voice remained steady.

He gently took my hand and inspected the small but painful wound. His eyes looked into mine with a mixture of concern and anger. His hand sent small electric currents straight to my nether regions, effectively minimizing the sting of my wound. A shadow crossed through his gray irises.

"We are done for the day. Let's get this cleaned out before it gets infected." He spoke gruffly.

"I'm fine. I'll clean it once we get back to the office." I gritted my teeth.

I sulked the whole way back to the office. I couldn't believe I was that stupid. I jumped down from the truck and slammed the door. I hadn't gotten halfway to the office door before my arm was pulled behind me. The sheer velocity of the force spun me around. I rammed into the strongest male body ever. Nash felt as though he were carved from granite. I didn't dare move a finger, even though they itched to run across his rock-hard chest.

I stared wide-eyed into the raging storm that brewed in his eyes. He brought my wounded hand up to his lips and whispered a kiss on the delicate skin above my cut.

"Better?" he huskily asked.

With my tongue tied in knots, all I could do was shake my head with acknowledgment. His kiss sent my body in overdrive: a live wire chock full of electricity. He cleared his throat. My hand slipped from his grasp as he stepped around me and straight to the office. I stood in the parking lot, dazed. Going inside was not an option. Dangerously sinful emotions whirled and twisted around my insides. I bypassed the office door and climbed into my car. I had to clear my head before I could even think about facing him again.

I drove straight home and gathered up the file on Gray. I programed her parents' address into the navigation system. The drive flew past my windshield as my foot defied the law's speed limit. This road was hardly ever on the cops radar. So, I took a little more liberty with the gas pedal. I pulled a right onto the gravel road that led to their home. Huge wide oaks lined each side of the long winding drive. Their mammoth branches loomed over the drive like a canopy. The fall weather had brightened the drive with the orange and red hues of their fallen leaves. The damp ground had turned the fallen leaves into bronze colors that matted the gravel drive.

I parked in front of the plantation-styled house. It had to be over a hundred years old. I wondered where their money came from. *Was it passed down through generations or had they bought the home later in life?* Gray's father, Harold owned a landscaping business. From the information in the file, it was extremely profitable. However, was it profitable enough for the large home and the land it sat on? The land was vast and I wondered how many acres there were in total. Her mother, Penny, was a stay-at-home mom. She had volunteered at the school library two days out of the week. She hadn't stopped even after the disappearance of her daughter.

I knocked on the large oak door. White paint chips scattered to the ground. I stood off to the left and gazed at the lush green grass that surrounded the house. Maybe I'd have to ask Harold how he accomplished that. All I could get to grow were weeds and crabgrass. I'm sure it took a lot of time and effort to maintain the lush greenery. I didn't have the desire to work that hard on my lawn. It was a small patch and I let it do its own thing. I wasn't home long enough to let the neglected look bother me.

The weathered door opened and I turned my

attention to the woman peering out. Her long, mousey-brown hair was pulled into a harsh bun. A few gray hairs sprouted along her hairline. The floral housecoat was faded from multiple washes and frayed at the bottom. It looked as though she had worn it every morning for years.

"Can I help you?" she asked in a timid voice.

"Hello. My name is Skye Briggs and I work for Donovan Investigations. May I come in and speak with you and Mr. McCullum about your daughter?"

Her hesitation signaled the alarm bells to go off in my head. If my daughter had gone missing and someone was here to talk about her, I'd have flung the door open and demanded that they tell me everything that they knew.

Her eyes remained rooted at my feet. "My husband isn't home at the moment. Do you have a card? I will call you when he gets home and you can come back then."

I dug in my purse, pushing around the contents until I found the slim business card holder. I plucked a couple of them from the case and handed them over.

"Thank you for your time."

She shut the door. I stood rooted in the same spot, hoping that she would change her mind and let me in. When it felt like five minutes had passed, I gave up. I walked back to my car, discouraged. I looked in the rearview mirror one last time. A curtain in the front window had fluttered. I was certain that she had watched to make sure that I had left. I shook my head at the mother's odd behavior.

CHAPTER 4

"WHY WOULDN'T SHE WANT TO talk to me? What if I had new information pertaining to her daughter? I just don't understand." I blew out a strangled breath.

I was beyond confused. I couldn't fathom any reason as to why she didn't want me there.

"It doesn't matter why she didn't let you in. She had her reasons. All you can do is wait for her phone call."

"What if she doesn't call?"

"Call his business and find out their hours of operation. Give him plenty of time to get home and settled. Then go back out there and try again."

"What if that doesn't work? What then?"

"One step at a time, Briggs. You won't solve this in a day's time. You don't have to wait to talk with her parents. You can talk to her friends, other family members, etc. Sometimes you can get more useful information from non-family members. Use all of the tools available until everything is absolutely exhausted."

I uncrossed my legs, preparing to stand.

"How is your hand?"

His gentle question kept me rooted to the chair. My cheeks warmed all over again with the memory of his soft lips. "Getting better by the minute. Thank you for not berating me over the mistake."

"Skye, I think you already know that I would never do that. You know all the reasons why it's important to go through each step over and over again. Practice and more practice will eliminate most of those errors. Muscle memory is what we are going for. We will go again when you are healed. If I am unable to take you, Ryker or Hawke will." His eyes lit up. "Actually, there is an outdoor range not far from here that we will go to. It will be good for all of us to partake in some field training."

"Sounds ominous."

"Just a safe place to blow shit up."

His face masked over. I already missed the grin that had made his features less intimidating. It drove me crazy not being able to tell what he was thinking.

"I'll let you know if I get a call back and what my next move is."

"Keep me aware of where you are at all times."

My eyes widened. "Do you think I will encounter trouble?"

I was so naïve.

"No, but it's better to expect it then to be caught off guard if shit goes down. That includes any case you take. Most of the jobs we take are laid-back but when you are dealing with people, some situations can go south real quick."

I pondered that for a minute. The only self-defense training I had was pushing strangers out of my way on Black Friday. Don't knock it; they are some of the ruthless people you'll ever meet. The deals weren't that great either. The one year I had ventured out was for a TV for my ex. He took that with him when he left four days after Christmas. All I had to show for it were some bruises and a wounded pride. I rubbed my sides as though they still ached. I had stood for hours in line for that damn thing. I wasn't about to let someone snatch it from me.

My reaction in a threatening situation would be unpredictable. I had no formal training like the rest of the guys. I was halfway down the corridor when I turned back around.

"Do you think I should take some self-defense classes?"

Nash looked up from whatever file he had been reading. "Wouldn't hurt. Or you could ask Ryker and Hawke. There is a full gym downstairs that you have yet to utilize."

Surprise kicked me in the gut. *Did he think that I needed to work out?* I know my jeans were getting a little tight but only when I washed them.

From his office, I headed straight to Ryker's. He was the lesser of the two evils. He had his phone pushed against his ear so I welcomed myself inside and sat in the chair opposite of his desk. I took the liberty to scan his space. The walls were barren. The small space was sparsely furnished and just plain drab. The natural light spilling from his lone window brightened the place immensely. He was lucky. My office could be mistaken for a supply closet.

"What's up, Briggs?"

I jumped in my seat, startled. I hadn't realized

that he had finished his call.

"Would you teach me self-defense?" I asked timidly.

He sat straighter in his chair. He was all business. "When do you want to start?"

Crappy doodles. I didn't expect that. I had hoped he'd brush me off. "Whenever you have free time."

He flipped through his calendar. "How about Tuesday evenings and on Sundays?"

I pretended to open up my calendar app on my cell phone, knowing full well that my schedule was wide open. I looked up at him. "I can work that in. What time?"

"Around five on Tuesday and eight in the morning on Sundays."

"Seriously, that early on Sunday? Can you do, oh, more like noon on Sunday?"

"You're funny. Nope, that's what I got. You can go ask Hawke if those days and times won't work." He chuckled.

"Nope. Not necessary. Those times will work fine. Thanks."

I hustled my ass to my office. I slammed the door behind me and leaned against the frame. My breaths came in pants and not because of the short walk to my office. Thinking about working out with Ryker had my adrenaline and heart rate up well beyond its physical limit.

Describing Ryker was hard. He spoke more than Hawke and gave off a more easy-going vibe. He reminded me of the actor Vin Diesel, with his deep baritone voice and rippling muscles. He literally scared the piss out of me. He would more than likely toss me around like a ragdoll. Two days out of the week, I would get my butt kicked. I hoped that Ryker would go easier on me then Hawke. My reproductive system wouldn't be able to handle Nash. Intimate holds, half-naked bodies, and sweat would have my system on overload. There was no telling what I would do in Nash's arms. I snatched some paper off the printer and fanned myself. *Lordy, it's hot in here!*

I glanced at the time and grabbed my shit. It was time to start talking to some of Gray's friends.

A toddler's cherub face poked out of the door.

"Hi, is your mommy or daddy home?" My voice sounded higher pitched than normal.

Kids weren't my forte. I liked them well enough, just not enough to spawn any. Her little pudgy fingers opened the door wider as she screamed for her mom. I cringed and willed away the urge to cover my ears. That was a prime example for not wanting any kids of my own. They only knew one pitch and it was the ear-piercing octave.

A perfectly coifed brunette walked toward the door. Surprise radiated throughout my system when I glanced over her perfectly styled hair and makeup. There were no bags under her eyes from sleep-deprived nights. Her clothes didn't have any little kiddo stains either. I had the silliest fantasy of her wearing an apron and an oven mitt over one of her hands. I sniffed the air. The atmosphere was void of baked sugary goodness. *What a shame.*

"Can I help you?"

Her voice was kind of snippy. Susie Homemaker could take a little more instruction from the Stepford wives.

"Hello. My name is Skye Briggs and I work for Donovan Investigations. I'm looking into the case about Gray McCullum. I wondered if I could talk to Rhana for a minute?"

Her cold gaze thawed a smidge when I had mentioned Gray. "Come in and I will get her."

I nodded my thanks and stepped inside the cleanest house I've ever seen. I had the overwhelming urge to take my shoes off. I didn't out of pure principle. I thought when you had children your house was in constant disarray. *Did she employ a maid?* After all, I was in the higher end of a middle-class home. I shut my assumptions off. *What the hell did I know! One thing for sure was that I was out of line and being a complete ass.* She led me into the kitchen, which boasted high-end appliances. I wanted to whistle at the glimmering space. The room was spacious with espresso cabinetry and light-colored, cheery walls. Much like the rest of the home, it gleamed with cleanliness. Not even one dirty little fingerprint could be found. Not that I would, mind you, but I could eat off of this floor. I pulled out a chair that had been pushed up against the table. I wiggled my butt, surprised at the chair's comfortable cushion.

A bubbly Rhana flew down the stairs. I could hear the pounding of her teenage feet against the hardwood stairs. I hoped her feet were bare because hardwood floors became slippery suckers when socks were introduced. I couldn't tell you how many times I've slid across my mother's floors with my socks. I could faintly hear her yelling at me to stop before I broke a leg.

She pulled out a chair and sat opposite me at the kitchen table. Her heart-shaped face and lovely cheekbones momentarily mesmerized me. Her genuine smile enhanced her youthful beauty. She was a spitting image of her mother. The resemblance was uncanny. I bet if I looked at pictures of her mother at this age, Rhana would look exactly like her.

"Hi, Rhana. I'm Skye and I would love to talk to you about Gray."

Her lips pulled down at the mention of her friend. "Um, sure. What do you want to know?"

"How about you tell me about your friendship so I can get to know her a little bit."

I didn't want her to hold back from me. I hoped that by letting her simply talk about her friend that she would inadvertently give me some helpful information. It was important for her to feel as though she had the control and that this wasn't an inquisition.

Her smile brightened once again. "Well, she really liked being at school and always seemed happy when she was there. She'd make jokes and make me laugh. I didn't know her as well as I would've liked."

I smiled encouragingly. "Did you hang out with each other outside of school?"

"No. Her parents were pretty strict. They didn't allow her to come over here. As far as I know, no one was allowed over there. Not that she had ever asked me over or anyone else."

"Did she ever talk about her home life to you?"

I was more curious about that than anything else. Her mother had acted strangely.

"Not really. I don't know much about them. She seemed close to her mom."

Her statement took me by surprise. "What makes you say that?"

"During lunch period, she would take her lunch to the library on the days that her mom worked." She turned her head to the left and then to the right before she spoke in a softer tone. "I love my mom but I wouldn't want to spend my lunch with her. It's kind of like a free period and I'd prefer to spend it talking with my friends."

I smiled and nodded. It made perfect sense to me. I loved my mother too. Although my eighteen-year-old self would have to agree with Rhana.

Rhana shook her head and the air around us turned melancholy. "She never missed meeting her mother. Even on the day that she disappeared, she met with her mom. She never returned to class and that was the last time I saw her."

I placed my hand over hers. "I'm going to find her. I promise."

Her eyes sparked with hope as they searched mine. I hoped to hell that I didn't let her down.

"Thank you for speaking with me. You've helped tremendously. I'm going to talk with your mom for a minute." I placed a card in her hand. "If you remember anything at all please feel free to call me."

"I will."

Her mother walked through the kitchen as Rhana exited.

"Thank you for allowing me to speak with your daughter. Do you mind if I ask you a couple of questions?"

"Not at all. I hope you find her. If this had happened to Rhana or any of my other children, I don't know what I would do. It's a mother's worst nightmare." Her eyes glistened.

"I don't have any children but the thought of this happening to anyone makes me sick." I cleared my throat. "Do you know much about Gray?"

"I honestly think that I know less about Gray than Rhana does. What I do know is from what Rhana has told me, which isn't much. I have only talked to Gray's mom a handful of times. Mostly, I kept trying to talk them into letting her come over for cookouts and birthday parties. To which, were all answered with 'No, thank you. We are busy.' I know that Rhana really liked her and was disappointed when Gray couldn't come over."

"Did that seem odd to you?"

"It did at first and then I just assumed that they kept a tight leash on her. I didn't agree with it, but then again, I am not her mother. I think it's important for your child to have some kind of social life. Be it sports or hanging out with their friends. I'm heavily involved in what Rhana does and with whom she hangs out with. So, I don't see a problem with letting her do certain things as long as she keeps up her grades and doesn't get into any trouble."

Mrs. Anderson looked down at the dainty watch on her left wrist. I got the message. She had other things that she needed to get done.

"Thank you, Mrs. Anderson, for your time." I

stood and handed her my card. "If you can recall anything, please feel free to call."

She nodded her head and walked me to the door.

I marched into Nash's office and plopped into the chair opposite his desk. I huffed out a loud sigh when he didn't immediately acknowledge my presence. He patiently put his file down and looked over at me.

"What's up, Briggs?"

I dramatically waved my hands in the air. "I don't know. I just got back from one of Gray's friends and I feel like I'm starting from scratch. They gave me zilch."

"They gave you zilch?" He repeated my statement in the form of a question, as though he hadn't quite heard me correctly.

"Exactly. Nothing."

"Why don't you stew over the conversation for a bit before you conclude that they gave you nothing of importance?"

Classic dismissal. "Great idea. I'll stew on it for a bit."

I huffed out of his office and traipsed toward mine. Nash wasn't going to hold my hand through this. I knew that, but for some reason the feeling of rejection loomed over me. It was an irrational feeling. My expectation for solving the case quickly was ridiculously high. This case wasn't in the same ballpark as tailing cheaters. The stakes were much higher. Giving closure to her family one way or another was the important factor. I couldn't imagine losing my daughter and never knowing what had happened to her. Living with the hope that she might come back one day or be found was a special kind of nightmare.

Gray would be graduating from high school this year. I couldn't comprehend why her mother had basically shut the door in my face. Another thing that bothered me was the fact that she remained a volunteer at her daughter's school. I'm not sure I could surround myself in the same halls she had walked every day as well as the same students who had been her friends. It would have been a constant reminder that my daughter wouldn't have the same opportunities as these kids did. She wouldn't attend prom, obtain her learner's permit, or walk across the stage for graduation. I wouldn't meet the man she would marry. I would never have any grandchildren. The list was endless. I just couldn't wrap my brain around this and I hadn't even skimmed the surface.

I combed over the notes that I had taken and let the conversation play through my mind. I had to give Nash credit. He was right. They had given me more questions than answers. With a case like this, I wasn't sure how I was going to find those answers. I had a feeling that her friends from school were not going to be of any help to me. More than anything, I wanted to go talk to Mrs. McCullum. She was the last one to see her alive.

I glanced at the clock. It was just after five. By the time I got out to the house, Mr. McCullum should be home from work. I put my notebook back into my purse and walked out of the office.

"Make sure you carry your piece," Nash stated as I walked past his office.

I did an about-face and stomped back to my office like a petulant child. I clipped my leather holster to the inside of my waistband. My new Kimber Ultra fit snugly into place. I hardly ever carried so the holster felt cumbersome. After the debacle with the Walther, I promptly went to the gun shop and traded the Walther out for the Kimber. I admit that the Kimber felt a whole lot more comfortable in my hand than the Walther did.

This time as I walked by Nash's office. I called out, "Thanks, Dad."

"Briggs," he growled.

Only a minor dig, but it sure as heck gave me the giggles. Knowing that I had gotten under his skin made the drive go quicker. I turned in to the scenic lane. Its imagery was quite different as dusk loomed on the horizon. The bark on the trees reflected vibrant orange hues from the setting sun. It was a breathtaking sight. I could almost breathe in the earthy aroma of fall. I rolled down my window and inhaled the crisp air. The ghost of summer slipped past my lips as I exhaled. An involuntary shiver racked my body as I hit the button to close the window. I wasn't quite ready for the winter chill that would promptly follow.

I parked my car in front of the house. I expected a warm welcoming glow coming from the rooms inside. Instead, a gloomy house loomed before me. The feeling of emptiness and loss radiated from the structure. I wondered whether it came from the occupants inside or the house itself.

The click of the motion light turning on could be heard as I ascended the porch steps. Darkness hadn't completely settled in for the night, so the light could barely be seen. I knocked on the worn wooden door. As I waited, I looked around. Unlike the yard, the house had seen better days. It was in desperate need of repainting. Chips of paint had floated to the worn porch. An old scarred bench swing hung on for dear life by one single rusted chain. The other chain lay limply on the floorboards of the porch. I imagined Mrs. McCullum rocking Gray as a young child for hours on that swing. I bet that spot was one of her favorites. It was a shame that no one bothered to take care of it.

I banged louder on the old door. Flakes of paint clung to the heel of my palm. I wiped my hand on my jeans. Half of the flakes transferred their hold to the material of my pants. The rest of them held fast to my skin. *This shit was like glitter.* No matter what you did, you'd never completely get rid of it. I let go of the nasty glitter issue for now and concentrated on the silent house. There had been no movement that I could hear from inside. I could sit on the porch steps and wait for one of them to come home or I could call it a night and go home.

A cool breeze blew across my skin. It was now pitch-black out and the temperature had dropped drastically since I had first showed up. A musty smell permeated the air. A pending storm was coming. *Screw it.* I loved a good storm but not while I was driving. I'd rather enjoy it from the comforts of my couch. I ran back to the car. If I hightailed it out of here and sped home, I'd make it before the first drops of rain could make their way down from the atmosphere.

I made it to the two-lane highway in record time. I kept the pedal to the floor. I blared the radio and sang off key. *Damn it!* I happened to look in the review mirror and caught the flashing blue and red lights. *Shit.* I slowed the car down and pulled onto the shoulder. I grabbed my license and registration. I rolled the window down and held the documents halfway out and gripped the steering wheel with my right hand. I knew the drill. This wasn't the first time I've been pulled over and it wouldn't be the last.

"License and registration."

His tone was light but all business. I twitched my hand in response. He took the papers and went back to his vehicle. I drummed my fingers against the wheel while my mind drifted toward the McCullum house. *What could Mrs. McCullum be doing this late at night?* I got the feeling that she was home every night, waiting for her husband to arrive. That was the vibe I got when I met with her the other day. But then again, I didn't know squat because she wouldn't talk to me.

"Do you know why I pulled you over?"

I jumped when the cop spoke. I hadn't realized that he had walked back to the car. I looked up into a young man's face. He was fresh off the academy line. Bless his cuteness. Of course I knew why I had been pulled over. *What kind of question was that?* I wanted to say something smart but I didn't think that this guy would think that I was funny.

"I was speeding, Officer." My lips twitched from holding in my grin.

"You were going twenty miles over the speed limit." He handed me back my ID and registration. "Slow down. Next time I won't be so lenient."

I looked down at the warning. "Excuse me." *Shit*. I had said that out loud.

"Would you rather me give you a ticket? Because I can do that."

"Oh my gosh, please don't." A nervous giggle bubbled out. "I thought you were going to give me a ticket. I certainly deserve one. I know I was speeding." *And insert foot.*

Seriously, why wasn't I shutting my mouth? I literally slapped my hand over my mouth, forcing myself to shut the hell up.

His deep chuckle resounded through my ears. The richness of his laughter flowed through me. I wanted to hear more.

"Slow down. See you around, Miss Briggs."

I rolled up my window and coasted back onto the asphalt. The rest of the drive home was foggy and driven well under the speed limit. That would have been a hefty fine that I couldn't afford to splurge on.

I unlocked the door while thoughts of the cop floated through my mind. He was a cutie but way too young for me. However, if I did run into him again, I wouldn't be opposed to some good 'old-fashioned flirting. Flirting didn't equate to dating. Although the title of cougar had me shaking my head while I laughed at the thought. *I was close to ten years older than him. Would I be considered a cougar?*

CHAPTER 5

I SUBMERGED MYSELF IN THE QUIETNESS of the empty office. It had been that way since I walked through the doors this morning. I had no idea where the guys were. It was rare for all three of them to be out. I was only mildly curious as to their whereabouts. The only sounds in the stillness of the morning came from the ticking of the clock and the hum of my printer. I had printed out the names and addresses for a couple of customers of Mr. McCullum. I also had a list of all relatives to the family. The list of kin wasn't nearly as long as I expected. Penny had one sister, who lived in Florida. Her parents were deceased and she had no other siblings. Harold's parents were in an assisted living facility an hour south of town. He had no siblings.

With my sidearm in place, I flung my bag over my shoulder and headed out. This early in the morning, the freeway traffic would be light. I became a tad aggressive when the freeway became chaotic with heavy traffic. My patience wore pretty thin with the stupidity of the other drivers. I swear the majority of them couldn't pass the driver's test to save their life. I turned the volume up and listened to my favorite XM radio station. I couldn't imagine going back in time to commercial-laden radio stations. It was almost as bad as TV commercials. I recorded all of my favorite shows so I could fast-forward through the commercials. Commercials rated high on my annoyance radar, almost as much as other drivers.

The drive through southern Indiana was spectacular and engaging. Most of Indiana was flat and basically filled with hundreds of cornfields. However, the farther south you travel, the more the terrain changed into beautiful rolling hills. The changing of the seasons brought images of campfires and s'mores to mind. The rich oak smell of burning wood and melted chocolate on my fingers brought back fond memories. When I was little, my dad would take us to Brown County and we would spend the weekend in a small cabin in the woods. While we fished, Mom would stay back and read. We cooked over the fire every night. My dad was the best storyteller. Some nights I slept with the sleeping bag over my head so the monsters in his stories couldn't find me. As I got older, the camping trips slowed down and eventually stopped.

There were beautiful horse farms to my right and I loved to look at them as I passed by. The split-rail fencing was enough to catch my eye. The pastures stretched as far as the eye could see. The dark black paint of the wood stood out, marking each distinct pasture with its lush green grass. There were times, like today, that I could catch a glimpse of the horses kicking and playing in the crisp morning air. If there were ever such a thing as reincarnation, I would choose to come back as a horse. Their honest nature and free spirit was something that I craved. Without sounding too cheesy, they were really majestic creatures. If I had the opportunity, I would plop my butt down in a pasture and bask in their tranquility.

I pulled into the nearly empty parking lot of the Sunshine Acres assisted living facility. The place probably sat on a wooded ten acres, which were semi-secluded from the main road. I didn't care for nursing homes but I could deal with this facility. I hoped to perish in a blaze of glory or at the very least in my sleep, before I reached the point of having to be put in to a nursing home. This place had a homier feel than most of the rectangular cinderblock and dreary buildings that nursing homes seemed to prefer.

I walked into a small, informal lounge area. Potted plants and other small shrubbery were strategically placed around the seating area. The Oriental rugs showed wear but still managed to brighten the entryway. To my left were three offices. I walked into the one that housed the director. At least, that's what the nameplate on the door said.

I politely knocked as I entered. *The door was open so I figured I had every right to breeze through, right?* A stout middle-aged woman lifted her head from the documents that she had been reading. She immediately took off her brightly colored readers.

She folded her hands on top of her desk and smiled. "Hello. How may I help you?"

"Yes. I am looking for Mr. and Mrs. McCullum. I was hoping you could tell me their room number." I returned her smile.

"I'll call up to their room. And you are?" Her pleasantries were still in perfect place.

"Skye Briggs, a friend of the family."

This woman didn't need to know who I worked for or what I was doing here. It was the family's business, not hers.

"Ms. Briggs, they are expecting you. Room thirteen in the B wing."

"Thank you."

She gave me the directions and I practically skipped out of her office. Her smile never left her mouth.

I walked past the dining area and the lingering smell of breakfast made my stomach show signs of life. I loved that the residents had the opportunity to come to the dining room and order a meal as though they were at a restaurant. It was a great place to socialize with the other residents. As I walked down the brightly lit hallway, the rooms were spread apart. I had assumed that they were built like hotel rooms, kind of all crammed in together. At the end of the hall, their door was the last one on the left. The one on the right was number fourteen. *How many wings did they have?* It was hard to tell how large the facility was from the front of the building.

I knocked on the door and waited. It didn't take but a moment for who I assumed was Mr. McCullum to answer.

"Hello. My name is Skye Briggs." I extended my hand.

He opened the door wider and shook my hand. "Tony McCullum. Please come in."

"Thank you." My smile was genuine.

I waited just beyond the doorway for him to take the lead.

"Come, let's sit in the living room. My wife, Samantha, is in the bedroom napping. I hope you don't mind that I don't wake her."

"Not at all."

I walked the short distance from the small kitchen to the living room. The kitchen was about the size of my bathroom, which wasn't large by any means. A small table separated the living room from the kitchen. I wondered whether that was done on purpose. The facility's method was to keep the kitchen small to entice the residents down to the dining hall that posed as a restaurant to allow their tenants to socialize. To my left, the door was closed. I assumed that was the bedroom. Their space was no larger than a hotel suite. For the two of them, it seemed cozy.

I sat on the loveseat while Tony took the recliner. I turned my body to face him and leaned my elbows on my thighs.

"What is it you wanted to talk about, Skye? I know that you are not a friend of the family."

And right to the point. This is why I loved the elderly. They never beat around the bush.

"Mr. McCullum."

"Tony," he interrupted.

I nodded my thanks. "I am a private investigator for Donovan Investigations. I was given Gray's case to look into. I wanted to come by and chat with you. Maybe try to understand a little more about her."

His eyes glistened with unshed tears. My heart immediately broke for him.

"We loved Gray so much. When Harold told us about her conception, we were thrilled. She was the light of our lives for so many years and when she disappeared, we were devastated."

I placed my hand over his. "I am sorry to have to be here in this capacity. I am trying my best to find her."

A small smile replaced the grimness of his tired-looking face. "I appreciate that and I hope you do find her." He leaned back in his chair and sighed. "We used to live much closer to them but with age and Samantha's short-term memory loss, I could no longer take care of her and our home. I decided it was best to move here so that I had help and yet maintained a semblance of independence. When we did, we didn't get to see Gray that much. She was about ten years old when we moved. We stayed in contact. She was such a caring young lady. She would call us every Saturday and chat for a bit."

"Would you say that you guys had a close relationship?"

"As close as it could be with the distance between us."

"I don't mean to be rude but an hour isn't that far to travel."

His chuckle sounded hollow. "I agree and had voiced that very thing many times. Harold would dismiss us by saying they would, but they never did. I could never wrap my head around why Penny didn't bring her by. I eventually quit asking."

"When was the last time you saw Gray?"

"I saw her about a month before she disappeared."

My mouth literally hung open. "I'm sorry, but you weren't on the list of people interviewed. Why do you think that was?"

"Probably because my son told the police that they haven't seen us for years and that she hadn't seen or talked to us in quite some time."

"But that wasn't the case."

"Well, for him, it was. Based on our conversation, I'd say that he had no idea we continued talking to one another or that Penny brought her to see us."

"Did Gray seem different to you when she was here?"

"Yes, but only in appearance. She had grown into a lovely young woman. She talked and laughed with us. She said school was great and she had some really good friends. I was happy for her and sad that I had missed so much of her life."

"How long did they visit for and do you know what their plans were afterward?"

His finger tapped against his chin as he became lost in thought. I sat on pins and needles waiting for his answer.

"They stayed for probably about an hour. I'm not sure what they were going to do afterward. I honestly didn't question why they had come. I was just so happy to see them. At the time, I thought that Harold didn't come with them because he was working. Now, I don't know what to believe." He sagged against his chair.

He deflated before my eyes. I hated to be the one to put more stress onto him.

"I only have one more question. Did you and Harold have a contentious relationship?"

"Harold was a good kid, albeit distant when he grew older. He worked hard to get his business off and running. Shortly after the birth of Gray, he immersed himself into the business. We helped Penny watch Gray when she was younger. I hate to admit this, but my son wasn't a very loving father or husband. When we moved, it was as though Harold used every excuse to keep her from us. He was busy and she was in school and they didn't have the time to visit. I could've drove up there but I got the feeling that he didn't want us there." He sighed in defeat. "There was always something that got in the way when I told him we were coming. Like I said before, I gave up asking and prayed that they would one day make it down this way."

I nodded. There was nothing that I could say to ease his pain. So, I kept my mouth shut.

I stood. "Thank you for taking the time to talk with me. I'm truly sorry about the circumstances." I pulled out one of my business cards and handed it to him. "If you can remember anything at all, please call."

He nodded his response and went to stand.

I held my hand up. "Please don't worry about walking me out. I can show myself to the door."

He looked as though he wanted to say something but held himself back. I took a chance at reading his thoughts.

"I'll let you know what transpires."

A small glimmer of hope shone through his glossy eyes.

I walked out to the car with a heavy heart and heavier shoulders. Inadvertently, Tony had given me a huge insight into their family dynamics. The information on Gray's disappearance eluded me. I also felt his hope weighing like boulders upon my shoulders. The same doubts crept inside my mind. *What if I couldn't find her?* I shook my head, loosening the negativity that tried to attach itself to my brain. I couldn't afford to keep letting those thoughts float around unsupervised. Otherwise, I would never solve this case. My insecurities would have to take a backseat and shut the hell up.

As I drove back to town, I couldn't help but think about Gray's family. *Why would Harold distance the family from his parents?* I couldn't understand why he had gone years without visiting his mom and dad. *Why didn't he know about Gray keeping in touch?* It seemed odd, especially when there seemed to be no overt division between them.

I drove through McDonald's and grabbed a large Diet Coke and a large fry. I was a sucker for both. The fries were the perfect size, with the right amount of salt. I would never turn them down, no matter how bad they were for me. I smiled and said thank-you as the young lady handed me my drink. The smile quickly faded when I screeched as the lid popped off the cup and the sticky soda spilled down the inside of my driver door. I managed to hold onto the cup, thwarting any more spilled liquid.

Thankfully, the lady had a bunch of napkins in her hand. I would need every bit of those and more. Their napkins were thin and didn't soak up much.

"I'm so sorry. Let me refill your cup."

I mean mugged her because what I really

wanted to do was scream. Not only was the side of my door still wet, but the left side of my pants. I took the freshly filled pop and gently maneuvered it to my cup holder. I looked down at the mess and noticed my e-cig sitting in a pool of the dark liquid. I rolled up the window and literally screamed. I better have a replacement. I was not going to the convenience store to buy one of the cheap ones that tasted like shit. I pulled out of the line and headed to the office. I had a spare set of clothes in my trunk and the office was closer than my house.

I was seeing nothing but red by the time I pulled into the parking lot. I ran up to the office and grabbed the Lysol wipes and a small wastebasket. I trotted back to my car, ignoring Nash as he called after me. Some things were more important than what the boss man had to say. It took me twenty damn minutes to get all of that cleaned up. My mood had not improved. I snatched my bag out of the car and trudged back into the office.

"Briggs, get your ass in here," Nash growled.

I rushed past his office. "I'll be there in a minute." I gritted my teeth.

I shut the door behind me and started stripping my soaked pants. I felt marginally better with them off so I turned my frantic mind toward the bag. I searched the pockets until I spotted one of my replacement e-cig. Thank God I had the forward thinking of ordering two and kept one in my bag. I hoped the battery had enough of a charge. I twisted it in place and took a puff. As the nicotine coursed through my veins, my body instantly relaxed. *Ah, that's the ticket!*

I lazily turned my head at the sound of the door. "Briggs, I told——oh. Uh, shit."

I was still a little high from the nicotine, so my reaction to being pant-less wasn't the same as Nash's, which was pretty damn comical. I was far from naked. My shirt hit the top of my underwear line. I wasn't even wearing my sexy panties. I had on a high-waist, muffin top slimmer. I've never seen or heard that man stumble with his words or his body. I couldn't hold back my laughter.

"Take a picture, Nash. It will last longer." I giggled.

When he slammed the door shut, I straight up donkey laughed until my gut hurt and tears ran down my face. When I was mostly composed and entirely clothed, I stepped out of my office.

I strolled into Nash's office with more confidence than I have ever felt while in his presence. His stuttered reaction had made him more human through my eyes. My shoulders were posture perfect and my head was held high. I had his gift of embarrassment in my back pocket and you bet your last dollar I would use it in the future.

"Hey, boss. You needed to speak with me?" My voice quivered slightly with barely contained humor.

He looked everywhere but in my eyes. Giggles were about to blow through the surface of my barely controlled persona.

"How's the case going?"

Instantly I was in business mode. "I drove down and talked with Tony, Harold's father. I found out something quite interesting."

His gaze finally found my eyes and his

embarrassment from earlier was now history. "Are you going to make me guess?"

I smiled. "Not at all. Tony had a visit from Penny and Gray about a month before she disappeared. We both concluded that Harold had no clue that Penny went down there. Also Gray had called them religiously every Saturday up until her disappearance."

His eyebrows rose. "That is interesting. What are your conclusions from the conversation?"

I crossed my legs and settled farther into the cushion of the chair. "The family dynamics are a bit odd. Harold seems to be a controller and believes that his wife and child should follow his instructions. He is a workaholic. His relationship with his parents is lackluster at best. Gray had kept a line of communication open."

"You are paraphrasing your interview. That is not what I asked you. What do you honestly think so far from the information that you have gathered?" he interrupted.

My eyes got as big as saucers and excitement bubbled beneath the surface.

"Something smells fishy. Maybe Harold had something to do with Gray's disappearance. I think Penny knows something. What that is——is what I plan on finding out."

"Good work. Trusting your gut is important. Keep digging."

"Thank you. I'm heading out to speak with one of his clients, Glen Parker. Have you ever heard of him?"

"Can't say that I have."

"All right. I'll catch you later."

CHAPTER 6

MY SECONDHAND MINIVAN CRUISED DOWN the quiet street of Glen's neighborhood. All the homes were built in a quaint cottage style. Some of the lots were larger than the others but for the most part, the small neighborhood teetered on uniformity. The homes were smaller than what you would picture on a waterfront. In the summer, I could feel the warm sun caressing my skin as our neighbors gathered for a block party. Faint screams of delight from the children rang in my ears as I envisioned them running and playing.

My phone chirped, bringing me out of my daydream. I swiped the screen, allowing the husky voice to rattle through the car speakers.

"What are you doing?"

My cheeks raised and I could feel the lines around my eyes crease. I adored this woman. She was the root cause of my many sessions of belly laughter that turned into sidesplitting pain. We hadn't known each other long and yet it felt as though it had been a lifetime. There are some people in this world that you just connect with easily. She was one of them. There was literally no work to maintaining our friendship and it was a beautiful thing. We spoke our mind with each other. There was no second-guessing or any mind games. If she or I were pissed, we let the words fly. Here is the thing: we have yet to piss each other off. That's how low maintenance we were. I cherished our friendship more because of that.

"On the waterfront, getting ready to ask a guy some questions."

"Sounds interesting. Is this one of your cheating bastards?"

"No. Thank God. Different case Nash handed me."

"I think we need to meet for drinks and discuss Nash and of course this new case."

"For the purpose of the case, I'll meet you at my place around seven."

"I'll bring the alcohol."

"Good, because I don't have any."

She chuckled. "You never do."

"Later, girl."

"Later."

I ended the call in time to make a quick right on to the cobblestoned drive. The house was cute with its royal-blue siding and white trim. The outside greenery was neat and well taken care of. I got out of the car and briskly walked up the narrow path to the door. I climbed the steps, onto the small porch, and knocked.

I could hear heavy footfalls nearing the door. I stood straighter and waited for the door to open.

"Can I help you?"

"Mr. Parker?"

"Yes."

His demeanor changed from slightly curious to

abrasive. He didn't seem to trust many people, me included. I wondered whether this neighborhood attracted many solicitors.

"My name is Skye Briggs and I work for Donovan Investigations. I am not here to sell you anything, merely to ask you a few questions." I looked into his weathered face, silently pleading with him to let me in.

His bushy eyebrows rose inquisitively. "What do they pertain to?"

"I would like to ask you about Mr. McCullum."

He looked from side to side, maybe to make sure that no one was within hearing distance. I couldn't be certain about that.

"Come inside."

Paranoia seeped from his skin and smacked me hard in the face. I had second thoughts about going inside his home, alone. *Shit!* I had yet to have a session with Ryker. I'd have to rely solely on my solid kick to the groin move. I stepped across the threshold already contemplating my exit strategy. I walked a couple of steps behind him, never taking my eyes off his movements.

"Would you like some coffee or tea?" he asked with his back to me.

"No, thank you."

He turned and held out his arm. "Please, take a seat."

I took the chair closest to the front door. The chair made a screeching sound as it slid across the tiled floor. I cringed as the sound assaulted my ears. He took his time preparing his coffee. So, I leisurely scanned my surroundings. The kitchen was small and tidy. The cherry-colored cabinets stood out against the cream-colored walls. I could tell it had been updated recently. Every surface glistened.

I watched him make his way to the opposite chair. He set his mug on the table before he sat down. He wasn't old by any means. He was probably in his fifties. It was his receding hairline and overly wrinkled face that made him look much older.

"I'm sorry about my abrupt behavior before. You had caught me off guard." He wrapped his hands tightly around the coffee mug. "What do you want to know about Harold?"

His admission surprised me. I wondered whether he knew more about the McCullum family than he had let on.

"How do the two of you know each other?"

His eyes went up and to the right as he contemplated his answer. "I had a landscaping project I wanted done and he was recommended to me by a coworker. At the time he was just starting out and did a good job. So, I thought that I would throw some work his way. He was young and eager. Hell, we all were."

His smile increased the longer he contemplated his earlier days.

"When did you commission his work?" I broke through his nostalgia.

"The first time was about eighteen years ago. He does projects for me from time to time."

"How well do you know Harold? Would you say that you are friends?"

"I would say that we are more acquaintances than friends. We play cards once in a while down at the golf club."

"Have you ever met his family?"

"No. I never have. I know about Gray's disappearance, which I presume is why you are here."

"What are your thoughts on Gray's disappearance?"

He ran his fingers through his thinning hair, making it stick up in various places. I wanted to lick my hand and smooth the hairs back into place. He didn't seem to notice that my gaze had become fixated on the top of his head.

"I really don't know. I've never asked Harold about it. Everything that I know is from what I read in the newspapers. The police had questioned me a long time ago and I didn't have anything information for them either."

"Do you think it's possible that she ran away with a boyfriend?"

"It's possible, yes. But I don't think that she did."

"Why is that? She was plenty old enough to have one."

"Harold was pretty protective over his family. As far as I know, they rarely left the house. That's just rumors, though. Then again, he rarely talked about his family to me. When I'd see him in town or at the club, his wife and daughter were never with him."

"Do you think that his protectiveness might seem a bit odd?"

"Isn't every family odd in some way or another?"

I thought for a moment before I answered his question. He had a valid point. My family could be deemed peculiar to an array of people and it felt completely normal to me.

"You make a good point. However, you have known Mr. McCullum for eighteen years. Don't you think in that time he would have mentioned his family or have at least seen them around town?"

"There was one time when he had told me that his wife was pregnant. He was overlyjoyed about the prospect of having a child. He was hoping for a boy. I had congratulated him and the conversation turned to other subjects. I had bumped into him at the nursery awhile after that and had asked him how his wife was doing and he had said that the baby was fine."

"That's all he had said?" I interrupted. Curiosity was killing me.

"Yes. I didn't ask anymore after that. He had made it clear that the topic wasn't open for discussion. I figured if he wanted me to know something then he would tell me."

"What do you think of Harold?"

"He is a talented landscaper and a very private man."

"Did he seem shaken or distraught when his daughter went missing?"

"If he was, he didn't show it."

I held my hand out to shake his. "Thank you, Mr. Parker, for your time." I took out one of my cards and left it on the table. "If you can think of anything, please call me."

"I will."

I slammed the car door shut. Frustration coiled in my veins. *What the fuck was going on with this case?* I blew out a breath and grabbed my e-cig. I put the car in reverse as I puffed away. Nicotine enveloped my frustration, allowing me to think beyond what people were telling me. There were so many holes in this case. I began to wonder whether I would ever find out what happened to Gray. I felt as though a child hyped up on sugar had taken a hold of my brain and used it as a merry-go-round. I couldn't make sense of anything. When the little sugar addict decided to stop the spinning, I knew I was going to fall on my ass.

I put the gearshift into drive and clicked the hands-free button on my steering wheel so I could talk to Nash. I was a decent driver but when I held the phone to my ear, I'd lose the ability to be animated.

"Boss."

"Take the rest of the day off. You've got a busy morning tomorrow," he barked.

"What's tomorrow? Do we have a meeting? Because it's Saturday and I planned on sleeping in." My hand automatically rose up in the air.

"Ryker asked me to fill in on Sunday. I can't do Sunday, so tomorrow morning it is."

My voice ratcheted up a notch, slightly panicked. "What do you mean Ryker asked you to fill in?"

"You have a problem with me training you Briggs?"

Damn his bossiness and damn his voice for making my southern region fill with desire. I slammed my hand on the steering wheel. I shut down my inner slut before I answered.

"Nope. No problem."

"See you at seven in the office gym."

"Got it," I huffed out.

"Don't keep me waiting."

He ended the call and my skin heated all over again. I blasted the air conditioning even though it was a cool sixty degrees outside. It took the whole drive home before I finally cooled off. *He was going to be the death of me.* I would spontaneously combust from all of the raging hormones he ignited.

I stood with the fridge door halfway open and stared at the miniscule contents. There was nothing but a tub of buffalo chicken dip. I turned my head toward the open pantry door. As I had feared: no tortilla chips or crackers. My bestie and I weren't beneath eating the dip with a spoon.

"Hey, bitch! Are you hungry?" Jackie hollered.

I laughed heartily and shut the fridge. Food wouldn't magically appear.

"Starving. I hope you brought food with that alcohol."

I met her halfway and hugged the snot out of her. I had missed her. We always got caught up in our own lives. Sometimes it would be weeks before we had a chance to catch up with each other. The infrequent visits didn't matter. It always felt as though no time had passed between them.

I held her at arm's length and grinned. "Jack Daniels, my girl. Do I smell Chinese?"

She twisted away from me. I knew she hated me calling her by her full name. It bugged the shit out of her. She liked to be called Jackie. So I made sure I called her that every chance I got. I chuckled as she beelined it to the kitchen to set her goodies on the counter.

"I got a bottle of wine and the best Chinese in town. I got to work early in the morning so I only bought one bottle."

"Good idea. I have to go in too. I wasn't planning on it either. Kudos for your smart thinking."

Jack was the opposite of me in every way. She had jet-black hair that hung in soft ringlets down her slender back. I could kill for her hair. She was runway perfect. She could eat whatever she wanted without even the slightest tip of the scale. I envied that. Hell, I looked at a damn donut and my hips instantly became larger. She was a strong and independent woman; that, for some, would be easy to be jealous of. I, on the other hand, marveled at the way she knew who she was. She made no excuses for the things that she said or did. You either liked her or hated her. There was no in between. When you got to know her, she was fiercely loyal to her friends.

She owned her own decorating business. Her eye for details was amazing. We had met a couple of years ago when I had my little abode decorated. She was just starting out and I didn't know what the fuck I was doing. I think I was more of a charity case in the beginning. She took pity on my lack of taste and fixed my house up better than I could have ever dreamed. Since then, her business has flourished. Now, I would never be able to afford her services even if I had three jobs and worked amateur night at Busty's Strip Joint. I loved watching those DIY shows where they renovated homes. Jackie would give them all a run for their money. She had the innate ability to surround you in tasteful pieces that were specifically tuned into the client's personality.

My home looked chic but not sterile. She had created a window bench in the office so I could curl up and read my smut. It was my most cherished place in my home. She introduced me to colors that I would normally never have chosen out of fear of it looking hideous.

"Come on, dig in. We don't have all night. We need to get this night started."

"Adulting sucks."

She rolled her caramel-coated eyes. "Preaching to the choir."

We sat on the couch with our feet propped up and our plates in our laps. In the silent living room, you could hear our collective sighs as we took our first bite.

"Tell me how hot Nash is again," she mumbled around the food in her mouth.

I almost choked on my sesame chicken. "You've met him."

"Yeah, but it's been months since I've seen him in person. I need my Nash fix."

I groaned. "I've got a training session with him in the morning. It was supposed to be with Ryker but he bailed. I don't think I can handle him touching me without trying to jump him."

She inhaled sharply. "I'd love to spar with him, Ryker, and Hawke. All three at the same time, preferably." She fanned herself.

"Get a hold of yourself."

"Hell, no. They are the only men who could probably tell me what to do and get away with it."

"Ryker and Hawke intimidate the hell out of me."

"That's because of all that muscle. Nash gets your girly juices flowing and that's the only reason you're scared of him."

"I'm not scared of him," I spat, a little defensive. "I'm terrified that I'm going to cross the line and get my ass fired. I need this job."

"Quit being a baby. You'll be fine. He is going to work you over so bad that your thoughts will only be of ways to kill him."

I chuckled nervously. She was right. I had a feeling that I wouldn't be able to walk afterward and it wouldn't be from the exercise that haunted my dreams.

"What's the case you're working on?"

I blew out a frustrated breath. "Do you remember the missing girl from a couple of years back. Gray McCullum."

"Vaguely."

"Well, Nash assigned it to me. I am beginning to wonder if it's solvable."

Her eyes enlarged. "No, shit. Really? He gave you the case?"

"I know, right? It's hard to believe. When he handed it to me, I thought I was being punked."

"You got this. You are the best person for the job. You won't quit until you find answers. You are good at what you do, Skye. I know he can see your talent. Otherwise, he wouldn't have trusted you with this."

"Thanks. This case is beyond my comfort zone. Cheating husbands are easy."

"That's why he gave you this case. To test your limits and to see what you are capable of."

"I guess. Anyway. What job are you working on now?"

It was time to change the subject, to get the focus off me. The way her eyes lit up, I could tell that she was excited about this client.

"If I land this deal, this client will set me up for the years! We are talking about seven thousand square feet of top-to-bottom revamp."

I squealed. I was so happy for her. She deserved it.

"It's in the bag. You'll land the contract and make a butt load of money."

"You know that's not what it's all about but it does make things easier." She chuckled. "I'm not overcharging him. I've made a fair bid and the family will love what I do. I have some finishing touches that I need to make before Monday's meeting."

We finished every tasty morsel on our plates as well as the deliciously sweet bottle of red. I hadn't felt this relaxed in forever.

"We need to make it a point to do this at least once a week," I loosely commented.

It never happened quite that way but she nodded her head in agreement.

"I've got to get going. Thanks for the company."

I got up and walked her to the door. She slipped on her heels before she hugged me good-bye.

"Thanks for the wine and dinner. If not for your

forward thinking, I'd be starving and parched."

"I know what's in your kitchen and that ain't much! Talk to you later." She held her hand up in a backward wave.

"Later."

I picked up the trash and put the leftovers in the fridge. They would make a good lunch tomorrow––that is, if I could quit picking at it all night. I loved Chinese food. I could eat it for three meals a day and never get sick of it. That and buffalo chicken dip. Hence, the reason they were the only contents in my fridge at the moment.

CHAPTER 7

I KEPT GLANCING AT MY WATCH as I drove to the office, afraid that I would be late. I didn't want to know what Nash would do if he was pissed. It was a wrath that I didn't want to experience. The sun had barely risen and here I was going to get a workout in.

I had to fight a yawn as I entered the gym. When my eyes landed on Nash's perfectly sculpted butt, my body instantly came alive. He was bent over, rummaging in his bag. I took my time ogling him without his knowledge. His body was toned in all the right places.

"Are you going to stand there all morning?"

I cleared my throat, embarrassed at being caught. "Yes, sir. Um, I mean no, sir."

His chin trembled as he tried to hold back his grin. He sat on the mat as I drew near. He motioned me with a nod of his head to sit next to him.

"We will stretch and get warmed up before we begin. It's important to stretch so that there are no injuries."

I nodded. Every fool knew that tidbit of wisdom. It didn't mean that anyone followed any of it. I imitated each one of the stretches. I knew most of the maneuvers from my brief stint with a personal trainer. I wasn't interested in sweating or puking for better health. I quit that venture that very day. I had a feeling that Nash wouldn't give a shit about my aversion to exercise.

Case in point: he started for the treadmills. "Quit stalling and get your ass over here."

Dejectedly, I hung my head. *Fuck!* I regretted waking up this morning. This was not what I had signed up for. I simply asked for self-defense moves. Frankly, I find this whole setup a bit over-the-top. The minute I spotted Ryker, he would hear a few choice words.

I climbed on the torture device and set a slow speed. The belt moved at the steady pace between a fast walk and a slow run. Much like those senior citizen speed walkers who zip past you in the mall. Lost in my own thoughts, I trooped along.

Nash reached over and increased the speed. "What you are doing is not running. You look like a drunk hobbling home."

"Thanks for the visual. I don't critique your form."

"That's because you don't need to but yours needs work."

I was finding it harder to form words as I tried to draw breaths. "You--are--mean."

His deep chuckle fueled my anger.

"You only have five more minutes to go. Don't quit on me now."

I couldn't speak. All I could do was grunt while I focused on breathing. *Where the hell was that runner's high?* Surely I would be infused with a bunch of endorphins by now.

He reached over and slowed the speed. I did not run on asphalt or treadmills. I ran solely on caffeine and nicotine. Now was probably not the time to grab my e-cig! Slowly my breath returned to a more comfortable level and my heart rate dropped to a more normal beat.

I stepped off the treadmill and stood for a moment. When the dizziness faded, I reached for a towel and wiped my drenched face.

"Are you all right?"

I looked up at his relaxed face and instantly wanted to slap him. I kept my hands to my sides. "Yep. What else are you going to torture me with?"

Heat simmered beneath his eyes and then just as quickly disappeared. "Come stand in front of me."

I did as he asked and stood about arm's length from him. Butterflies sputtered deep in my belly.

"There are seven parts of the body that are the most vulnerable. The proximity of your attacker will determine which of those parts you will attack."

"Got it. Eyes, nose, groin, and knees."

"Don't roll your eyes at me. Get serious, Briggs," he growled.

I halted another eye roll. "Yes, sir."

He ran his hands through his hair and blew out a weighty breath. "You only named four. The other three are the neck, ears, and legs."

He maneuvered his body as close as he could without invading my personal space. Which was still far too close for my comfort.

"Pretend that I am your attacker. Bend your

fingers so that they touch the tip of the palm. Use the second knuckle of your fingers and jab at his eyes. You can also use the heel of your hand and ram it up at an angle. This will push his nose up and into an unnatural position." He shifted his weight so it was evenly distributed between his powerful legs. "Now I'm going to inch my way forward and you imitate striking my eyes and nose."

I cocked my head to the side, unsure of my aim. He advanced, the butterflies scrambled into frenzy, and I struck out. My knuckles connected with his eyelids with more force than was necessary. I felt him jump back as my knuckles connected with his fleshy tissue. I cringed from the squishy feeling and partly from the yelling that was sure to come. I peeked open one of my eyes and stared at the hunk before me. His nostrils flared and his jaw muscles moved back and forth. *Shit!*

I shrunk into myself as he stalked closer. His hands grabbed my arms and pinned them to my sides. In a split second, he twisted me around so that my back slammed into his front. My breaths came in short pants. His arms wrapped around my torso, effectively caging me in. My heart rate sped up as adrenaline pumped furiously through my blood. I knew logically that he wouldn't harm me but my body was in full flight mode. A hint of a doubt had planted its seed in my brain. I was scared to death. I had hit him harder than I meant to. *Was this his retaliation?*

"What is your next move, Skye?" His hot breath fanned across my neck as he spoke.

Neurons started to fire and my brain engaged.

I inhaled deeply and exhaled to control my next movements. I rocked my head back and barely touched the back of my skull to his. Then I bent my leg at the knee and brought my foot gently down on his foot. After that, I was out of ideas. His arms loosened and I could finally breathe normally.

"Excellent. That is exactly what you should do. Make sure you connect with the most sensitive body parts with as much force as you can muster."

I turned to face him. "I'm so sorry that I hurt you. I didn't mean to."

His grin transformed his threatening face back to handsome and the storm brewing in his eyes cleared. "I know but I needed you to be frightened. Your attacker will not stop. They will be relentless and you need to be ruthless."

"Okay, what's next?"

I hopped up and down on the balls of my feet, eager to learn more. His laughter rang out with a rich tone. Giddiness bubbled beneath the surface, knowing that I had earned a more personable side of him. I could definitely get used to that sound.

"I'll teach you how to get out of more difficult holds."

Yum, yes please!

Come to find out, the type of holds he executed were not the same as the ones I had envisioned. I was completely drained by the time that he had finished squeezing and contorting my body. I snatched up the towel that had been lying innocently on the floor. I swiped the towel along my sweaty face.

"Good job today. I'll let Ryker know what

we accomplished and he will tailor your next sessions."

I nodded, still mopping up my face.

"When you're ready, come up to my office and we will talk about the case."

I glared at his retreating back. He hadn't broken a sweat and looked as good as he did when I first walked into the gym. I know I looked wrung out. I didn't need a mirror to see it. I probably smelled like a sweaty gym sock, too. I desperately wanted a shower and fresh clothes but that would have to wait.

I felt sticky as I flopped down in the chair opposite of Nash. He looked at me with a glimmer of humor in his eyes. *Damn him and his exemplary physical fitness.*

"It's like she floated away. So far there has been no trace of her. There was no boyfriend. I can't come up with a plausible reason for her disappearance. Hell, I can't even wrap my brain around this one yet. I've only talked to the grandparents, one of Harold's clients, and a school friend of Gray's." Strands of hair should've moved from my face with the force of my exhale. The dried sweat had cemented them to my cheeks. "His client mentioned that Harold was a private person. Harold seemed excited about the baby but when Glen tried to ask how his wife was doing, Harold clammed up and never talked about them again, even though the two of them play cards together regularly. Her grandparents got a visit from Gray the day before she disappeared. Before that, it had been years. From what I gathered from his dad, Harold wasn't aware of their visit. I don't know——this whole thing smells fishy."

"Have you managed to talk with her parents yet?"

"No. I planned on going out there this afternoon."

"Do you want me to go with you?"

"No——Yes——I don't know." I sighed heavily.

I wanted to do this on my own but this was so beyond my expertise. A little handholding sounded nice. *Scratch that.* I could do this on my own.

I sat up straighter. "Not this time. I'll let you know if I need you."

He nodded his head in approval. At least I think it was approval. One could never tell with Nash. He could've been holding his breath from my stench.

CHAPTER 8

BY THE TIME I FINISHED freshening up and hit the road, it was late afternoon. My knowledge of running a landscaping business went about as far as my ability to find a missing girl. I still held out hope for finding the girl—forget the landscaping business. I hated to sweat and get dirt under my fingernails. I assumed that Harold wouldn't be home but I wasn't going to miss out on the chance to try to talk to his wife alone. I rolled down my window and enjoyed the rare warm weather.

I was closing in on their driveway entrance when blue and red lights flashed in my rearview mirror. *I guess I better pull over.* Hell, I was slowing down anyway. I was about to put my blinker on and get ready to turn anyway. I silently chuckled. Who was I kidding? I was out in the middle of nowhere and I wasn't about to use a blinker. I put the car in park, gathered my documents, and put my hand half out the window.

"Miss Briggs, we meet again."

I sensed the familiar smile in his deep voice. My eyes traveled from his state-issued uniform up to the creamiest mocha-colored skin. His strong jawline outlined a formidable face. Full lips cracked into a beautiful smile that showcased slightly crooked front teeth that I found adorable. His dark-brown eyes glimmered with mischievousness. He was beautiful in the most masculine of ways. I couldn't help the smile that spread across my face.

"It's good to see you again, Officer. What can I do for you?"

He chuckled. "For starters, you could abide by the speed limit that is clearly posted."

"I could, but then I wouldn't have had the pleasure of seeing you." I winked.

At least I think that's what I did. I could also be stroking out. Jack wasn't with me to ask her whether I was still smiling.

"You can put your documents away. I don't need them. This is your last warning. Next time, I will write you a ticket," he stated, driving his point home.

He tore off a slip of paper and handed it to me. I folded it and stuck it in my cup holder.

"Yes, sir. I promise that the next time you see me it won't be for a ticket."

"Have a good day, Miss Briggs."

I checked out his backside through my side mirror as he leisurely strode back to his cruiser. I bet he looked just as good out of his uniform as he did in it. I pulled back onto the highway and promptly put my blinker on to turn onto the McCullums' drive. Even if they were not home, the day wasn't completely wasted.

I knocked on air. The door flew open and I came face-to-face with a double barrel shotgun. *Oh, shit! I just dribbled in my underwear.*

I cleared my throat and stood tall, reminding

myself to show no fear.

"I'm Skye Briggs, a private investigator for Donovan Investigations. I'm going to reach into my bag and pull out my qualifications."

"I don't give a shit who you are. Get off my property. You are not welcome here," the gruff voice commanded.

I couldn't get a clear visual of his face due to the shotgun. I wasn't going to give up just yet. "Please, Mr. McCullum? I just want to ask you a couple of questions with regards to the disappearance of your daughter."

I was proud of the way my voice remained calm amid the turmoil that rolled in my stomach.

"I don't have a daughter. Now, get the fuck off my land and do not come back."

He cocked the shotgun; I twisted around and practically ran back to my car. In my head, I was doing a full-on sprint. My body moved with a swift cadence. With shaky hands, I started the car and got the fuck out of there, kicking up the loose stone on the drive in my wake. I slowed down when the house was no longer in view. I pulled to a stop at the end of the drive and put the car in park. I sat there until I calmed my nerves and most of the trembling had subsided. I pulled out my cell phone and dialed Nash's number.

"Briggs."

"Nash! That fucker pulled a shotgun on me. I didn't even get a chance to ask any questions. He told me he didn't have a daughter," I rushed out in one long breath most likely not making any sense to him.

"Where are you now? Are you safe?"

"Yes and I'm parked at the end of his lane, safely out of sight and shot range."

"Take a couple of deep breaths and then head to the office."

His take-charge and detached tone helped me gather my thoughts and settle down.

"I'm fine. I'm gonna pull out and head home. I'll figure out a way to talk to the wife alone. I'm curious as to why he had said that he didn't have a daughter. Do you think it's because he killed her?"

"I don't know. It's a possibility. Hard to say when he isn't accessible. I agree you need to question the wife when she isn't at home. Leave Harold to me."

I liked the idea of never having to speak to Harold again. He definitely was hiding something. I just needed to figure out what that something was.

"Let me talk to the wife first and then we will go from there. I still need to talk to her sister but that's not a trip I think I need to make yet."

"Let me know what transpires with her and then we will reevaluate."

"Thanks, boss."

"Be careful, Skye."

The worry in his voice actually helped extinguish the remaining fear. I smiled as I clicked the End button.

I drove the rest of the way home. Driving the recommended five miles over the speed limit. I wanted to push the pedal to the floor but didn't want to push my luck and get pulled over again. There was no telling how many freebies the cute officer would give me.

Speaking of cute officer, I pulled out the slip of

paper when I parked in my drive. The front was a blank citation. I flipped the sheet over and spotted the seven-digit number written in bold black ink. A goofy grin spread across my face. The crow's feet around my eyes etched deeper into my skin.

I stared at the screen of my phone for so long that I jumped when Nash rang through.

"Boss," I said a little leery.

"Briggs."

I found our short dialogue quite comical.

"I'm home." I shattered the silence first.

"You were supposed to call me when you got home."

I didn't have to be standing in front of him to know that he was angry with me. I imagined his strong jawline pinched shut with anger. His gray eyes looking much like an impending storm. I could almost feel the vibrations from his carefully controlled voice, warning me of its lethal strike. God help me, but I enjoyed pushing his buttons. Especially when I wasn't within arm's reach. A thrill went through me as I added a dollop of fuel to the fire.

"You never said that."

"I shouldn't have to. It was implied," he barked.

What I should've said was *I'm sorry. I misunderstood your instructions.*

"Are you worried about me, Nash?" That cheesy smile was back.

"Follow orders next time."

He abruptly cut off the call, ending any further teasing. I recalled our previous conversation and he had not told me to call him when I got home. As much as I tried, I still couldn't read minds. *Yep,*

I was softening him up. It only took me about a year. Maybe, this time next year, I'll have him sharing my bed. It's good to have goals.

I gathered my stuff and headed inside. I poured a healthy glass of cheap wine and settled in my reading nook. I had drunk three glasses of wine before I gathered up enough courage to dial the sexy officer's number. He would make a nice distraction while I waited for Nash to come around. I was about to hang up when his familiar rich voice came over the line.

"This is Omar."

And I had his name! It suited him and his creamy mocha skin.

"This is Skye."

"I wondered if you would find my number."

"I did and called you. Do I need to come to the precinct for traffic school?"

I could hear his chuckle through the phone.

"That might not be a bad thing, seeing as you have a problem obeying certain traffic laws. Of course, they have those classes online now for your convenience."

"If I learned to go the speed limit, then I would never have the pleasure of you pulling me over."

Oh my goodness, was I really flirting? It had been so long that I almost forgot how this little game was played.

"Good point. But next time, it might not be me who pulls you over. What I was really thinking was taking you to dinner tomorrow night. It's my night off and I would love to spend that time getting to know you."

"Let me look at my schedule."

I wasn't really looking at it. I didn't have any plans—at least not with a hot guy involved. "Would you be wearing your uniform?"

"Nope. You get boring old me."

"That's a shame but I guess I can make an exception."

"How about I pick you up at six?"

"How about I meet you at the restaurant just in case our date is a total bust and we hate each other."

"I can work with that. Let's meet at Steam Boat Lillies."

"Sounds good. I'll see you tomorrow evening."

"Have a good night, Skye."

"You too, Officer."

I immediately slapped my forehead for the dumbest comment ever. *You too, Officer, really! Could I be any cheesier?* I hit myself again for any future dumb shit that would inevitably come out of my mouth. A rubber band around my wrist would be a better deterrent. *Smack, smack, and smack, all day long!*

I grabbed the bag of pita chips and tore into them. I dipped a healthy dose of buffalo chicken dip. More dip than chip because that's how I roll. After I had consumed the whole container, I felt sick to my stomach. I rubbed my belly and then rolled off the couch. I took my gluttonous self to bed and ignored the alarm bells of vomit threatening to force its way out.

CHAPTER 9

"I'LL WAIT HERE ALL DAY if I have to," I hissed.

I yanked out a chair at the empty table closest to the front desk and plopped my ass onto the hard seat. Mrs. McCullum had nowhere to go. From my vantage point, I had access to all doors and the entire desk. She couldn't give me the skip. I didn't bother with introductions. She knew who I was from my previous two visits to her home. I was still fuming from my last encounter with her fuck-wad of a husband. She had been hiding like a coward. I had an innate desire to kick controlling men in their balls and slap a collar on them. I would love nothing more than to drag Harold down Main Street at the height of traffic and put him in his pathetic place.

I didn't walk in her shoes and I didn't live her life. Assuming what she had to endure day in and day out would make me the ultimate bitch. However, I was pissed that she and her husband were keeping me from finding answers. Which, in turn, made me care less about what she went through at home. Even if I got the beating of a lifetime, I'd still want to find my daughter. That was unless she knew exactly what happened to her.

I didn't blink the whole time I stared daggers at her. I sat and fumed as the minutes ticked by. I sat up straighter as she whispered to her coworker. I watched her every step, making sure that she continued to move closer to me. I looked up as she stood before me.

"There is a study room in the back. We can talk there." She motioned for me to follow.

We walked through aisles of books. I inhaled the aroma of the worn pages of the books that lined the shelves. I was tempted to run my fingers along their spines. The library was one of my sanctuaries, but today it felt lifeless. Maybe it was because the silence wasn't at all comforting or I was getting closer to the answers. I hated that my favorite place had turned into a nerve-racking nightmare.

I shut the door behind us and the sound of the click echoed off the walls. The small space held a desk and two chairs. The walls were white and sterile. The tan of the cheap wood closed in the room more. Mrs. McCullum sat heavily onto the chair. I took my time pulling out the scarred wood. Before I could sit, she spoke.

"I don't know what more I can tell you that I haven't already told the police."

Her body slumped as though the weight of the world rested on her shoulders. I pushed back her feelings of helplessness before they invaded my psyche.

I kept my voice clear and void of any emotion. I couldn't afford to lose focus. "I'm sorry that you are going through this. There is no greater loss than the loss of your child." I truly was sorry for her.

"Do not talk to me as though my daughter is dead. I know in my heart that she is alive," she snipped.

I deserved that. "Again. I am sorry. I didn't mean to imply——"

"What do you want to know?" She cut me off.

I sighed heavily. This was much harder than I had thought. Trailing people was so much easier. I could hide behind the camera.

I put my phone on the table. "Do you mind if I record our conversation?"

She waved her hand dismissively. *Damn if she wasn't a different woman when her husband wasn't underfoot.* I kind of liked this new side.

I pushed the record button and dove in. "Tell me about the day that Gray disappeared."

She laced her fingers in her lap and stared at them as she spoke. Her voice was subdued. "It was like any other day. It was my day to work in the library, so instead of dropping her off and heading home, I parked the car and walked into the school with her. I gave her a kiss as she went to class and I signed in and headed toward the library. About midway through the day, Gray had come and asked me to take her home because she wasn't feeling well. I took her home. I asked her if she wanted me to stay with her and she told me that she was fine. It was just a stomachache and to go back to the school. I made sure she was settled before I left. There were only a couple of hours left. I didn't need to go back. I'm just a volunteer, so it wasn't imperative if I returned. Gray knew how much I loved it there, so she told me to go and I didn't think anything of it."

She looked me in the face with glistening eyes. Then she turned looked around the room, seeing things that I had no idea of. I waited patiently, more like bit my tongue, and waited for her next words.

"You see, my husband is a controlling man. He never used to be this way. When we first met, he was so vibrant and full of charisma. It wasn't until after we were married and he began his landscaping business that things started to change. He was gone all the time and when he did come home, it was late and he'd just go to bed and it would start all over again the next day. This went on for a year. I couldn't stand to be home all day with nothing to do. We didn't have a lot of money at that time so I decided to go back to work. When he found out, he went ballistic. Saying that no wife of his was going to work, that the business was going to take off and he wanted me to stay and take care of the home. So I quit. I hadn't been working long anyway. It was just easier than listening to him scream at me." She ground her jaw together. "I know what you are thinking. But, I can assure you that he doesn't beat me and he never laid a finger on Gray. He wasn't the most loving father but he is still her father. Regardless, after Gray was born and went to school, I started volunteering for her field trips, class parties, and anything that I could to get out of the house. Unfortunately, my daughter witnessed our loveless marriage and his controlling ways. Most days, I felt trapped in that home when Gray was in school. The volunteering helped and my husband never said a word about it. I want my daughter found. She is my life and the only family I have besides my sister."

"I'm working hard on doing exactly that. Did she have a boyfriend she may have run away with?" I had to ask. I didn't believe that she did but it was worth a shot.

Her face scrunched up and bitter laughter spilled out. It wasn't the happy-muscle-cramping-laughter. It was laced with sadness and a touch of sarcasm.

"No. Gray and I were always together. She never went out of our home by herself. She had no one besides me. The only time I ever traveled was to my sister's and we haven't seen her in years. Even those trips were denied me. I drove her to and from school every day. She didn't have a cell phone. We don't own a computer except for my husband's laptop, and he keeps that with him and has a password so we don't use it. The only phone we have is our landline."

Harold was a piece of work. I wanted to know how someone who was initially excited about having a baby morphed into someone who treated them as if they were expendable.

"Didn't your sister come to visit you?"

"Once and she never came back."

"Why?"

"She never approved of Harold. She came to visit right after Gray was born. I asked her to be Gray's godmother. We were having a small baptism and she had come up for the weekend. Nothing important happened but Harold's demeanor destroyed any future visits."

"Who is her godfather? What about Harold's parents?"

"When they moved, we lost touch. I tried to keep in touch over the phone but we never went to see them. Technically, she doesn't have a godfather. The day of her baptism, I pulled Tony aside and asked him to fill in. He loves Gray, so I kept it that way, regardless if Harold approved or not."

She was lying and I knew that because I had spoken with Tony.

"What about any of Harold's clients?"

It was a long shot.

She shook her head. "We never met any of his clients. I don't even know who his friends are. I no longer talk to the ones we had when we first met."

"Was anything disturbed when you got home and noticed Gray not there? Were any of her belongings gone?"

"No. Nothing was taken and nothing was moved or knocked down. There was no struggle, if that is what you were asking."

"Did you lock the door when you left to go back to school?"

"Why would I? You see how far out we live. We are miles from our closest neighbor. She was sixteen and way older than most kids who are left alone. I trusted that she would be okay without me for a couple of hours."

I pushed the pad of paper in front of her. "Will you write down the names of your neighbors for me? I would like to ask them some questions too."

She pushed the pad back in my direction. "I can only give you the wives' names. The only reason I know of them is because they dropped off casseroles and such right after Gray went missing. Before that, I had never met them."

She turned her wrist to look at the face of her small watch. "I've got to go. School lets out soon and I need to finish helping."

I stood with her and gave her my card. "Please call me if you can think of anything."

She nodded and strode out the door as though flames were licking at her heels. I walked through the library quickly and headed to the office. I was relieved to bypass all of the school traffic. It would have been like leaving a concert early to beat the congestion.

I ran to my office and powered up the computer. I pulled up the yellow pages and went to type in the names that Penny had written down for me. My fingertips froze over the keys. *Shit!* She had only written down their first names. I knew it couldn't be that easy. *Nothing ever is.* I sighed, a bit overly dramatic. I pulled the case file out of my drawer and combed through the witnesses. I put the file back and slammed the drawer shut. "REALLY?" I literally shouted. *Who doesn't talk to their neighbors?* They usually see more than what close friends and family do. Everyone knows this. Apparently not everyone because they sure as shit didn't interview them.

"What's up, Skye?"

I jumped at the sound of his voice. "You've got to quit sneaking up on me. One of these days you're going to give me a heart attack."

"I doubt that."

Well, maybe not a heart attack but my ovaries were going to explode with all that heat he packed. "I forced Mrs. McCullum to sit and talk with me. She gave me the names of her neighbors but only first names. I can't look them up without their last names." I turned my chair around to face him. "This case is frustrating, that's all. I feel as though I am running headfirst into a wall at every turn."

"The tough ones always feel like that. It means that you are making headway. Keep digging and the answers will become more obvious."

I caught myself before I rolled my eyes at him.

"Trust me. I've been doing this a lot longer than you. My toughest cases were fought at every turn. What about the receptionist position? Have you found any candidates yet?"

I did roll my eyes at him this time. "No, I haven't found anyone yet. I've been too wrapped up in this case that I've forgotten all about it."

He slipped out of the office. Halfway down the hall, his voice boomed. "Then I guess you're going to have to pull double duty until then."

Son-of-a-bitch! He could hire someone himself but I promised him that I would if he gave me a chance at PI work. He made good on his word; I guess I would have to make good on mine. I quit the search for the neighbors; they were a dead end at the moment. I pulled out the file I had on the few resumes that had been sent. I placed a call to each applicant, making sure to set each interview up for tomorrow. It was short notice but the applicants didn't seem to have any conflicting obligations. The sooner I hired a receptionist, the quicker I could get back to the case.

I packed up and shouted a quick good-bye to anyone who was listening. Nash's baritone voice stopped me at the foot of the stairs. I swiveled and headed to stand in the doorway of his office.

"You going home for the night?"

"Yep. I've got a hot date to get ready for."

"Remember you've got training with Ryker tomorrow evening."

A maniacal laugh blew loudly through my head. "I haven't forgotten."

"When you are done with the interviewees, I want you to narrow it down to two possible candidates and we will do a second interview with them together."

I saluted him in the most comical way. I caught a twitch of his full lips before his features went blank again.

"Good-night, Briggs."

"Night, boss."

I exited swiftly before he had the chance to call me back.

CHAPTER 10

I TOOK MY TIME STYLING MY hair and picking out my outfit. I didn't want Omar to think that I was out to impress him, even though I secretly was. I chose a pair of boyfriend jeans that had the trendy rips in all the right places. I paired them with a V-neck white shirt and a three-quarter-length black jacket. I slipped into my closet and longingly looked at my favorite fur-lined Crocs. I shook my head and grabbed the black-heeled sandal that I wore once to a family wedding. I double-checked my image, made sure I didn't have anything hanging out of my nose or stuck in my teeth, and headed to the restaurant.

Steam Boat Lillies was only about a ten-minute drive from my house, but took me less than that. The restaurant was a decent place to eat. They prided themselves on their seafood but I thought it was overpriced for the quality. They did, however, have the best burgers—go figure. I walked in the door and scanned the seats, looking for Omar. I spotted him at one of the corner tables. I bypassed the hostess and walked toward the table. He stood and pulled out a chair opposite the one he had vacated. I did a quick scan and he was just as hot out of his uniform, maybe more. Which I found ironic because he looked gorgeous in his uniform. His presence was just as commanding.

I looked up into his chocolaty pools. My nether regions did an internal sigh. "Thank you."

His smile reached his eyes and it had a dazzling effect on me. *Holy shit, I was in trouble if one look had me weak-kneed. Let's hope he didn't screw that up when he opened his mouth.*

"What would you like to drink?"

The waitress appeared out of nowhere. I couldn't tell you what she looked like; I was still a little dazed. I snapped out of my fog when I heard her clear her throat. *Crap! He was letting me go first.*

"I'd like a Bud Light, please."

"I'll take a sweet tea."

"Would you like an appetizer?"

My gaze traveled over to my date. We both shook our heads.

"Great. Let me get your drinks and I'll be back to take your order."

"Do you——"

"How long——"

We both started at the same time.

"You go first." He chuckled.

"How long have you been on the force?"

"About seven years."

"Do you like the food here?"

I couldn't contain my burst of laughter. "I love their burgers. The seafood is okay but overpriced."

"Good. I hate seafood."

"Then why would you choose this place?"

"I saw it when I was out on patrol the day I had talked to you. I didn't want to give you a chance to say no, so that's what I blurted out."

The waitress butted in our conversation to take our order. We both ordered burgers with a side of fries.

"What's your last name?" I blurted as soon as the waitress left.

"Montejo. Are you going to do a thorough background check on me?"

The amusement in his eyes was boyishly charming.

"Nah, more like, making sure that my first name flows with it. You know, just in case. I'd hate for it to be Perry or something like that. Plus, I wouldn't want to pass down that kind of name to our children," I panned seriously. "Do you have a pen? I should start practicing my new name."

"As long as we have a big strapping boy named Jesus and a princess we shall call Juanita." He stared at me and then burst out laughing. "Or we could take on your last name."

"I'm kind of digging you right now, Officer Montejo." My lips trembled with the need to smile. "Taking my last name would be the less sexist thing to do. Let's try it out for effect. Omar Briggs." I sighed with sarcastic disappointment. "Nope. I'll have to take your name. It has a certain ring to it."

Bantering aside, I could tell that he enjoyed the gentle sparring as much as I did. The comical quips were fun and light-hearted. It had been too long since I had this kind of release. This was comfortable and yet the sexual undertones were electric. If we weren't compatible in the sack, which would be hard to believe, I knew in my heart that he would be one of my best friends.

At the moment, I didn't want to be his friend. I wanted more no-strings-let's-see-where-this-goes kind of relationship.

Around the next bite of his burger, he asked, "What is it that you do, besides speed?"

I swallowed. "I'm a PI. I work for Donovan Investigations. I've been there for a while. I started out as the receptionist and now work as one of the PIs."

"Why haven't I seen you around the precinct before?"

"Most of my cases centered around cheating husbands. I just started working on a missing persons case."

"How's that going?"

I sighed. I really didn't want to talk about it but I could tell that he was genuinely interested. "It's slow and frustrating. It's a cold case, about two years old. I more or less am fumbling my way through it."

"I'm not a detective and I can't imagine working that aspect of the force day in and day out. Those cases are like a jigsaw puzzle without a picture to work with. You keep putting the smaller pieces together until the big picture is revealed. I like mine to be cut-and-dry," he said matter-of-factly.

His confidence wasn't the suffocating kind; it was more of a soft caress. I soaked it up like a sponge dipped in a bucket of water. He was refreshing in every way. Time seemed to slip by without my notice.

The waitress walked to our table and set the check down. "I'm sorry, folks, but we are getting ready to close up."

"Seriously! Wow. I am sorry."

Omar handed over his card. "No problem. We will be out of your hair shortly."

"I can't believe we closed down a restaurant. A bar seems to be more fitting in this scenario."

"That can be arranged." He turned his smile up another notch.

"As much as I would love for this night to continue, I have interviews starting early in the morning."

He left a hefty tip and he guided me out. "Which car is yours?"

"The mommy van over there."

"Already thinking about our growing family?" A teasing laughter was back in his eyes.

I think I just fell in love. "You caught me. And here I thought I was being coy."

He leaned over and planted a soft, tantalizing kiss on my lips. It was merely a whisper, one that asked to be invited in. I kicked open the door and let him lead. The sensual kiss seemed to last for hours but most likely a minute in real time. I felt a sense of loss as he pulled away.

I licked my lips. *Yum. Better than the burger I just ate.* "Thank you for a wonderful evening. I can't remember the last time I have had such a good time."

He placed a stray strand of hair behind my ear. "I have to tell you that I'm not one of those guys who says he will call and doesn't. Especially when I've had a really good time. My next rest day isn't until the end of the week but I'm going to call you tomorrow."

"I'll answer."

"Good-night."

"Night."

I got in my minivan and drove away. I glanced in my rearview mirror and my lips curved into a smile, as he remained rooted in the same spot until I could no longer see him when I turned the corner.

CHAPTER 11

A TRIPLE VENTI FROM STARBUCKS AND I felt semi-amped to complete these interviews. I had enough caffeine running through my system that I should be able to fly through the potential candidates. *There were only four. How long could it possibly take?*

Amy Fisk was the first interviewee. She looked fresh out of high school, cute and petite. The boys would thank me if I hired her on the spot.

"Hello, Ms. Fisk." I extended my hand.

Her handshake was loose and noncommittal. I filed that away for later. I led her to the conference room. She sat in the chair with a straight back and her boney fingers clamped together tensely in her lap. Interviews in general sucked. I wanted to make her feel a little more at ease. Otherwise, I wouldn't get a real feel for how she would perform her job duties.

"Where did you grow up?"

Awkwardly, she cleared her throat. "Born and raised right here in town."

"A Hoosier like myself."

The blank look on her face solidified the fact that she was just a baby. Either that or I just showed my age. I chuckled inwardly.

I turned my attention away from Ms. Fisk when I heard the clicking sound of the door opening. Nash popped his head in and stole the rest of the oxygen that filled the room. I was used to his effect on me, so I ignored all of the tingling sensations wreaking havoc through my body. I sneaked a peek at Amy and burst out laughing. Her mouth hung open and her eyes were as round as saucers. She didn't even blink an eye at my outburst. I didn't have to guess what was going through her mind. Nash had the superpower to render a complete shutdown of the female mind. Every muscle liquefied, turning said female to a pile of hormone-filled goo.

"How's it going in here?" Nash's gaze never left my face.

Did he not see the beautiful young woman sitting across from me?

"Great. We were just getting started."

"Hi, Amy. I'm Nash."

He turned his lethal eyes toward Amy's already reddened cheeks.

Her eyelashes fluttered and she stuttered out a hello.

"Skye, when you are done, please come to my office."

The twinkle in his eye shimmered with silent laughter.

"Sure thing, boss."

I wasn't surprised that he knew that I was interviewing Amy. He had probably done a thorough background check on each of the applicants. Once the pheromones turned to a simmer, I proceed with the interview. Between her resume and the short answers that she provided, I knew she didn't have the experience needed for the job. I had a gut feeling that it would take longer to train her due to all of the male testosterone hanging in atmosphere. She would spend most of her time gawking. I stood to shake Amy's hand and thanked her for coming in.

"Thank you, Ms. Briggs. I look forward to hearing from you." A tentative smile formed across her innocent features.

I followed behind until I reached Nash's office. I strolled through the open door and shut it behind me.

I slunk down in the chair and waited for him to speak.

"That bad, huh?"

"I hate interviews. Even if I am the one conducting them."

"How did Amy do?"

"She's inexperienced and quite smitten with you."

"Will that inhibit her performance?"

"With the three of you around? Yes, I believe it will. She is also starting her third year in college. This would be a stepping-stone for her and she most likely will be gone within a year's time. I don't feel that we should completely take her out of the running but so far she is not my first choice. We still have three more applicants to go." I looked down at the face of my watch. "Speaking of which, I have another interviewee scheduled in twenty minutes. I want to go over the application before I sit down with them."

I crossed my legs on top of my desk and leaned

back in my chair. I scanned Lisa Barron's resume and felt confident that she would make a good receptionist. She was in her late forties, married, and recently heading back in to the work force. I took her resume and headed out to wait for her.

"Hello, Mrs. Barron. I'm Skye. Let's go into the conference room. Would you like anything to drink?"

"No, thank you."

Her voice held just the right amount of authority. Raising three children would have that affect.

"Please have a seat."

She carried herself confidently. As she placed her hands on top of the table I noticed a small tremor. She reminded me of a duck in water. Above the surface she was a picture of control but below the water, her legs moved with fervor. I smiled inwardly. She would need that façade while working in this office. The boys were intimidating enough to look at and more so when they spoke.

"Mrs. Barron, what made you decide to come back in to the workforce?"

"Please, call me Lisa. My boys are almost grown. Drake graduated high school last year and Levi and Lucas are juniors this year."

"Wow, twins! You seem so sane."

She threw back her head and let out a great peal of laughter. I wasn't entirely sure why I laughed with her but she was infectious.

She dabbed the corners of her eyes. "I wouldn't go that far. They've kept me busy for a long time. Now it's my turn to do something different."

"Have you always been a stay-at-home mom?"

"No. I met my husband, Matthew, while I was working at a local bank. I was the loan manager. He had stopped in to talk to me about a small loan and from then on we've been inseparable."

I smiled genuinely happy for her fairytale. "Raising three boys of your own will help you immensely around here. Nash owns the company and Ryker, Hawke, and myself are his minions. Being happily married will help you keep the drool at bay. These boys are a big slice of lusciousness."

A familiar deep chuckle could be heard from the now open door. "Mrs. Barron, it is a pleasure to meet you."

Nash had walked in at the worst time. He extended his hand to Lisa.

She cleared her own chuckle from her throat. "The pleasure is all mine, Mr. Donovan."

He nodded his head and motioned for me to follow him.

"Please excuse me for a moment."

"Take your time." Her devious smile reached her eyes.

I groaned as I followed him to his office. "What can I do for you, boss?" I sighed as I closed the door behind me.

"I want you to offer Mrs. Barron the position. I've done a thorough background check on her and come to find out, I know her husband. He has done some work on my car. They are a good family. They don't need the money but I know that she will work hard for the company."

"What do you want me to tell the other applicants who have yet to interview?"

"Go through the process and tomorrow let them

know that the position has been filled."

"You want me to waste their time?"

His carelessness irritated me. If I was going to hire Lisa then what was the purpose of proceeding with the interviews? Wasting their time and mine seemed counterproductive.

"The other two applicants are young and need the interview experience. You have nothing on your agenda today. I know you've already cleared the day to conduct the interviews."

I rolled my eyes. *Damn him and his telepathic ways.* Sometimes I really hated that he could read me like an open book.

"Fine, but I don't like it."

"You don't have to. Just do it."

In my mind, I flipped him off.

"I saw that."

I growled and slammed the door on my way out, knowing that would piss him off. I grinned all the way back to the conference room. *It's the simple things!*

Lisa looked over at me as I entered. The damn smug grin was still plastered all over her pretty features.

"Why do I get the feeling that you are rubbing that little encounter in my face?"

"Because, Skye, I am."

I laughed so hard that my cheeks burned from lack of use. "You are a breath of fresh air and just what this office needs." I extended my hand. "You're hired. How about you start tomorrow?"

Her grip tightened. "What time?"

"Eight."

"I'll be here."

"Great. I'll see you first thing in the morning. We will get all the paperwork signed and then get started on your duties. The job is full-time with benefits, from eight to four———Monday through Friday. Do you have any questions?"

"If I come up with any, I will bring them to you tomorrow."

"Wonderful. Enjoy the rest of your day."

"You too."

I watched her walk confidently out of the building. Nash brushed up against my arm, watching the same silent exit. The left side of my body tingled and heated with his closeness. I stepped away before I acted out the lustful thoughts that invaded my brain.

"Why don't you finish the interviews?" I was serious but the question came out more as a whine.

"It's your job."

I put my hands on my hips and cocked my head to the side. "You keep barging in as if you are the one doing them anyway. I've got a case to investigate."

His lips twitched. *God, he was so freaking handsome, especially when his humorous side tried to take over.*

"Good idea. As your last duties as secretary, you can bring them in when they get here."

"Fine."

That didn't go as I had planned. That meant that I was stuck in the office until they were over. I rolled my eyeballs toward the ceiling and prayed for them to be over quickly.

I sat out in the open at the secretarial desk and poured over my notes. Frank something-or-other, I really wasn't paying too much attention to him, cleared his throat. I greeted him and walked him to Nash's office like a good little girl. With Frank immediately forgotten, I sat back down at the desk and picked up where I had left off. Which was pretty much nowhere. There had to be something that I was missing. *Why the hell did Gray go missing? Who the fuck took her and why the hell couldn't I figure it out?* Her father was the key to this whole case. He had to be.

I had an idea. I pulled out my phone and did a Google Earth shot of Penny's address. There were two neighbors, about a mile apart on both sides. All I had to do was show up. I didn't need to know their names or who lived where. They were the closest and might be more helpful than everyone else I'd already talked to. I'd take a drive out there tomorrow. I wouldn't be in any shape after my session with Ryker.

I ran home to change into my workout clothes. I looked longingly at my bed. A nap would trump Ryker any day, but I didn't want to get my ass handed to me by Nash. I finished getting dressed, grabbed my water bottle, and headed back to the office. Just as I had put the car in park, my phone rang. I twisted in my seat and dug through my purse. *It's as though everything I throw in my purse disappears.*

Before the call ended, I swiped the phone without even looking at the number.

"'Lo."

"Hello, Skye. Did I catch you at a bad time? You sound hurried."

I sank deeper in the driver seat. "Nope, you

caught me at the right time."

"I did, huh?"

"Yep. You gave me a couple more life-saving precious minutes."

"That sounds ominous."

"It is if you were about to get your butt kicked by a man twice your size."

"Seriously? What the hell have you gotten yourself into?" His playful tone turned stern.

I laughed at the seriousness of his question. "Nothing like what you think. I'm meeting one of my coworkers. He is helping me with some self-defense."

"Good to know. I thought I might have to play the knight in shining armor."

His accent grew thicker as he joked. Goose bumps erupted over my arms.

"More like knight in shining uniform."

"That too. How was work?"

"Low-key up until now. Is your shift over?"

"Almost. I wanted to give you a call and see if you wanted to meet for a nightcap, but it seems as though you already have plans."

His voice held a hint of disappointment.

"I wish I could but this is my night with Ryker."

"Do I have some competition?"

Laughter straight from my gut erupted. "Hardly. You are still number one in the running."

I could hear his smile through the phone. "Good. Then I will see you this weekend?"

"Sounds like a date. I'll call you later on in the week."

"I'll talk to you soon. Have a good night and make sure you go for his balls."

"That goes without saying."

I ended the call with his laughter ringing in my ears.

I dragged my body through the office to the gym. I knew I was stalling but it was beyond my control to make my body move faster. My session with Nash was fun and invigorating. I had a feeling that Ryker would be out for punishment for having to teach me simple self-defense moves.

I walked into the gym and tossed my bag in the corner.

"You're late."

"Hello to you too."

"Being late tells me that you are not serious about your safety. If you aren't taking this seriously, you are wasting my time."

"I had a phone call right before I came in. I had to take it. Quit being a fucking douche bag."

"Hop on the treadmill and let's do a ten-minute warm-up. I've got a date tonight and I am not going to be late because you were busy gossiping."

I grabbed the sidebars before I turned my head to the side to look over at him. He was tough and built like a brick house but he was tense for some reason. I knew the cases that he was working on and they didn't seem to be that taxing. *What else could be causing him to be an ass?* He's normally easy to get along with.

"Oh, I get it. You are hoping to get laid and I am vagina-blocking you."

He kept his focus straight ahead. "Vagina-blocking? What does that even mean?"

"You know, like cock-blocking."

His steps faltered, getting caught on the belt of

the treadmill. If he fell off. I would have no choice but to hysterically laugh at him.

"You are something else, you know that?"

"Yes. Yes, I do. You will begin to enjoy it—sooner or later."

His slight grin was all I needed as an answer.

"Yeah. I actually set up this date before I realized that we had a session. Do you mind if we cut this short?"

Ah, now we were getting somewhere. "Not a problem."

What I didn't realize was that shorter didn't mean easier. For forty-five minutes, Ryker managed to toss me around like a rag doll. The sadistic look in his eyes confirmed that he enjoyed the hell out of it too. He looked refreshed walking out of the gym, while I looked as if I had been rode hard and put back wet, and not in a good way. My muscles ached in places that I've never even thought were possible. I wanted to crawl out of the gym but I had too much pride. I slung my bag over my sore shoulder and walked out of the building as though I had something shoved up my ass.

CHAPTER 12

I PUFFED ON MY E-CIG AS though my life depended on it. There wasn't enough nicotine in the world to help me forget about my aches and pains from last night or the fresh memory of a shotgun shoved in my face from a previous visit to the McCullums'. Their neighbors might love their guns too and I wanted my system pumped full of as much nicotine as my system could handle. *What the hell had happened to Southern hospitality?* A nice glass of sweet tea or lemonade would be a more welcoming gesture. Technically, Indiana wasn't the South but living in the country gave it the impression.

I was coming up on the McCullums' drive, so there was roughly two miles left before I needed to turn in to the neighbors drive. Before it was said and done, I would know this road like the back of my hand. I didn't mind the drive. Out here, other cars were sparse and it gave you the illusion of being miles from civilization. *If only the cornfields could be replaced with oaks and rolling hills.* I loved my town but the flat terrain was uninspiring. I put my blinker on even though there wasn't a soul behind me and turned into the gravel drive.

The driveway was short and the worn

farmhouse came into view. Just beyond the home was the biggest barn that I have ever seen. It had to have cost more than the home and probably housed expensive equipment. Probably one of those enormous tractors that cost more than I would make in five years. I parked in front of the weathered two-story. Before I had the chance to open my car door, a woman with a blue apron stood on the porch with her hands on her hips. I got out of the car and headed straight for her.

I extended my hand. "Hello, I'm Skye Briggs and I work for Donovan Investigations. May I speak with you about the disappearance of Gray McCullum?"

Her stance wasn't aggressive in nature so I took that as a good sign. Her head angled to the side as she sized me up.

After a brief hesitation, she shook my hand. I sighed inwardly with relief. All that nicotine had my heart racing.

"I'm Nancy Grieves. Would you like some water? We can sit out on the porch."

"No, thank you. I appreciate you speaking with me."

She guided me to the right of the worn porch, where two rockers sat. "I don't think I can tell you much about Gray or her disappearance. We are neighbors but we don't know each other."

I silently rocked while I thought about my questions. "Your farms butt up against each other, right?"

"Yes, they do. Our land meets with their property on the south side."

"Have you encountered the McCullums at any

point?"

She nodded her head. "Yes. We have occasionally met in passing. They seem to be a private family. There have been no problems with them. During harvest season, we rarely see anyone but the family."

"Have you ever spoken with Mrs. McCullum?"

"Once or twice but that is about it. Our conversations weren't lengthy. The standard generic and impersonal conversations you have with people you hardly know."

I nodded, knowing full well how those conversations went. Working in sales required the mind-numbing exchanges.

"What about the neighbors on the other side? Do you know them? Do you think that they were friends of the McCullums?"

Her answer was automatic, not even a halt in her rhythmic rocking. "No. The Williamses live on the other side of them and they are in their early eighties. They don't venture out much."

"That doesn't mean that they don't converse with Mrs. McCullum."

"Probably not, but they go to my church and I've known their family most of my life. They used to own the McCullums' property but when they started getting up there in age, they decided to sell most of the land and the big house. They live in what used to be another barn that they converted into their living space. Their grandkids are the same age as my boys and go to the same school. I would have heard if they had any kind of relationship with them."

"Did they go to school with Gray?"

"She was a couple grades ahead of them. So they wouldn't have known her."

I pushed myself out of the rocker, turned to face her, and shook her hand once again. As much as I enjoyed sitting here, I wasn't getting any new information. This was another dead end. I was beginning to think that Gray was a ghost. If it weren't for the other witnesses, it was as though she never existed.

"Thank you for taking the time to speak with me. Do you mind if I gave you my card in case you remember anything at all?"

"Not at all."

I walked back to my car, crushed with disappointment.

I turned my car back onto the main road and headed back to the office. I glanced in my rearview mirror and saw flashing lights. *Shit, not again.* I pulled onto the shoulder and gathered my information. With my hands at ten and two, I waited for the officer.

"License and registration please."

My heart skipped a beat as the familiar accent hit my senses. His voice sent shivers down my body. I smiled wickedly up at him.

"Officer, this might be considered harassment. I had my cruise set to five miles over." I couldn't help but tease him. He was so damn sexy in his uniform.

He leaned his muscular arms on the open window ledge.

"Provoking an officer comes with consequences."

Holy shit! The consequences might be worth it. I gazed into his deep chocolaty pools and was suddenly famished. I was hungry for his touch.

"And what might those consequences be?" I asked breathlessly.

His minty breath whispered across my lips. "I might have to use restraint."

A breathy moan escaped my lips as I imagined handcuffs and his hard body sliding over mine. For once in my life, I didn't have a comeback. My mouth slightly parted, waiting for him to fuse his silky lips to mine. In the blink of an eye, he answered my silent plea.

Anyone passing by would think that Omar was in trouble. His upper body was inside my car while his lower half remained on the asphalt. I'm sure it looked more like a scene from a sci-fi flick, but that's not where my thoughts were. My mind was only concerned with the way that his soft lips felt fantastic against mine. His tongue was doing a wicked dance, making me think of another area that needed his expertise. His hands tightened around my hair and the pull went straight to my southern region. His mouth swallowed my moan as pleasure radiated throughout my body. I needed him to relieve the ache and douse the inferno.

The intensity of his kisses faded as he pulled back. My fingers trailed his jawline as he pulled himself out of the window until only his strong forearms were planted on the window. The fire he had ignited was now in smoky ruins. I wanted to throttle him and eat him alive. It was fine line between lust and anger. The mischievous grin that adorned his chiseled face was enough to cool me off further.

"You are not playing fair, Officer."

I could've called him by his name but I was still miffed enough to childishly withhold it.

"Neither are you. My pants are uncomfortable at the moment."

I sadistically laughed at him. I was thrilled that I had the same effect on him. "Do we have to wait until this weekend?" I pouted.

"My shift ends at seven. You want to pick up where we left off?"

"Absolutely."

He leaned in again and placed a chaste kiss upon my lips. "I'll bring dinner. See you soon."

I watched as he strutted back to his cruiser. His backside was just as sexy as his front and tonight I planned to see all of it.

CHAPTER 13

"I'M RUNNING OUT OF LEADS, Nash. I can see why the police never solved this case. It's impossible."

"It's not impossible. You are tenacious and you will find the answers that you are looking for. I gave this case to you because I know you can solve it."

"Are you sure? Because from where I'm sitting, the situation sucks."

I was rewarded with a chuckle and I immediately loved the sound of it. Knowing that Omar was coming over tonight helped squelch the desire for my boss that continuously simmered below the surface. Nash was excellent eye candy but today my fantasies waned enough so that I could concentrate on our adult conversation.

"Completely."

"I might need to take a couple of days. I'm going to talk to Gray's aunt. She may know something. It's a long shot but I feel it's worth taking."

"Do you want company?"

His comment completely threw me off my axis. *Did I want him to go? Would I be able to survive the trip?* Nash would be by my side and in close proximity for the entirety of our trip. It's one thing to fantasize from afar but up close and personal for several days might be my undoing.

"I'll leave it up to you," I said, unable to mask my surprise.

His face was a blank slate. *Was I supposed to say yes, I want you to come or no, I've got this?* If Ryker or Hawke left out of state, Nash wouldn't think twice about asking to tag along unless they as a team decided that the threat warranted backup. I wanted to ask him whether he thought that I couldn't handle this on my own. I knew better than to ask and I didn't want to know his reasons for offering.

"I'll have her make the arrangements tomorrow, after I've looked at my schedule. When were you wanting to leave?"

"I was thinking first thing on Monday."

"I'll let you know tomorrow if I'm going or not and I'll have Lisa email you your itinerary."

"Thanks. I'm going to pull some data on Diane, see what the background check reveals."

"Make sure you get out of here at a decent hour tonight."

I grinned from ear to ear. "Oh, I will. I've got a date."

His eyebrows raised a fraction, indicating his surprise. Normally, I kept quiet on my dating life but I was so ecstatic that I could hardly contain myself. I hoped that my dry spell would be eradicated tonight.

"Enjoy your night," he growled.

I ignored his snarkiness. "You bet your sweet ass that I will!"

I probably shouldn't have said that. But damn,

he did have a sweet ass.

I had about an hour before Omar arrived. I put away the information that I had gathered on Diane, which wasn't much. She was Penny's only sibling. She was a couple of years younger than Penny and had never been married. She had no children and lived on the Florida east coast. With the chilly fall, Florida sounded glorious. Warm weather, sun, and sand. It would be easy to say fuck it and make it an extended stay. I could already feel the gritty sand attaching to the soles of my feet. The doorbell rang, lifting my hazy daydream.

I opened the door and my smile broadened in approval. Omar stood, seemingly pleased with himself after my eyes had devoured his body from head to toe. His brown eyes met mine and contained a sensuous flame that had my toes curling. He closed the gap and placed a gentle kiss to my cheek. My hand flew to where his lips had seared the delicate skin.

I cleared my throat, trying to remember my manners. "Whatever food you brought smells delicious."

"I wasn't sure if you liked barbecue or not."

I peered over my shoulder. "Who doesn't?"

Amusement flickered in the mocha-colored eyes that met mine. "Not any friend of mine."

"I'm glad we are on the same team." My voice held a trace of laughter.

"Me, too."

His laughter was low, throaty, and warmed every inch of me.

I wanted sustenance but I wasn't sure my need for Omar outweighed my need for the delicious smelling barbecue. *Screw it!* One great thing about barbecue was that it could be eaten cold and would remain every bit as flavorful. I took the bag of food from Omar and set it on the kitchen table. I turned back toward him and the heated look in his eyes scorched my body.

He slowly stalked toward me. The closer he came, the less air I could draw in to my lungs. His powerful, well-muscled body commanded the air between us. He reached his hand up and lightly fingered a loose tendril of hair and placed it behind my ear.

His free hand moved recklessly to my neck and drew me closer. I barely knew this man. My head shouted expletives down to my southern region. My hormones had built an impenetrable wall from their frenzy. Every word that my brain shouted bounced off and was lost in the sea of lust as his lips pressed against mine.

Through my haze, I could faintly hear the incessant ringing of a phone. I ignored it until the cold air hit my senses once Omar had pulled away from me.

"I have to get this." His voice was hoarse with frustration.

I bit down hard on my lower lip to keep me from saying something that I would regret. I wasn't entirely convinced that I was upset with the interruption of his phone. I liked him and enjoyed his company. He sent my body into overdrive every time he was near but something was missing and I couldn't put my damn finger on it.

A shadow of annoyance crossed his face. "I'm sorry. I have to go. There was a pileup out on the interstate and I've got to go in."

I shuddered inwardly at the thought of all those people hurt—or worse. "Of course. Call me later if you get the chance and please stay safe."

My hand involuntarily moved toward his cheek. He turned his head toward my palm and placed a searing kiss.

"Thank you for understanding."

I dropped my hand and watched him walk out.

He looked over his shoulder. "Just so you know, I am having one hell of a time walking out this door right now."

I smiled but didn't answer.

I didn't bother with a glass as I snatched the bottle of wine. I stalked straight to my reading nook and flopped down. A comedy and a good buzz was the remedy that I needed.

CHAPTER 14

BANG, BANG!
What the fuck! I shot out of bed and practically slid down the stairs in my stocking feet. I bypassed the door and headed straight for my gun lying peacefully at the bottom of my purse.

BANG, BANG!
My fingers slipped from the handle. *Shit!* I reached for it again. With an unsteady grip, I held the pistol to my side as I walked to the door. I peered through the peephole. *Fuck!* I released the breath that I had been holding and unlatched the chain.

"Holy shit, Nash. You about scared the piss out of me. I could've shot you!"

I waved the gun around carelessly. He grabbed hold of my hand that held the cold metal and expertly removed the piece from my manic grip and slipped it into the back of his waistband.

"You can have your gun back after you've calmed down."

"Calmed down! Calmed down!" I screeched. "You're the one who escalated this whole scenario with all of that pounding. Is there an emergency or are you just plumb fucking crazy?"

Lust simmered in his gray eyes as he stalked

toward me. I retreated slowly, unsure of his next move or of his motives for pounding on my front door this early in the morning. My heartbeat accelerated and a bead of sweat lined my upper lip. My clit contracted as he encroached my space. My back hit the wall, halting any escape. His steely arms caged me in. My chest rose with excitement as he leaned closer. His lips brushed the side of my ear. They were but a mere whisper that caressed my entire body. His leg rested between my thighs and I desperately wanted to rub myself against the hard muscle.

"Are you done?" His gruff voice sent my hormones into a passionate turmoil.

I could only nod.

He grazed his teeth along my sensitive lobe and I moaned with pleasure. I wanted to touch and dig my nails in to his back but he had my arms pinned with the weight of his perfectly sculpted body. I stood frozen, completely turned on, and wanting him to tear off what little clothing I had worn to bed last night.

"Go put some clothes on before I break every promise I made to myself when I hired you." His lips kissed their way down my neck to my collarbone. He stepped back and pinned me with his storm-ravaged eyes. "It's time to go interview Mr. McCullum." He stepped farther away and started for the door. "I'll wait for you in the car. Do not take long or we will miss our window."

I remained against the wall, trying to catch my breath.

"Skye." He looked over his shoulder with a pained look.

He shook his head and walked through the door as my silent pleas——for what, I don't know——shattered my reality.

I was falling head over heels for my boss. *How pathetic was that.* He clearly stated that there would be no relationship between us, regardless of the sexual tension. He was right. I couldn't date my boss and I couldn't quit my job. I wasn't seasoned enough to go out on my own, especially not with Nash as competition. Even if I quit and we screwed each other's brains out, that didn't ensure that there was any kind of longevity for us. It was time to put my big-girl panties on and ignore my feelings for him. I mentally slapped my brain for such stupidity. I would continue to harbor feelings for that damn-sinful man despite the million reasons why I shouldn't.

Gravel spit out from our tires as he gunned the car down Harold's drive. We pulled up and blocked his car so that he didn't have an escape. We stepped out of the car as soon as Harold barreled out of the house. The slamming of the screen door echoed through the air. He rushed toward us with a crazed look in his eye. I glanced over at Nash and saw that he had his hand hovering over his gun.

He stopped within a few feet of us. With his arm outstretched and his finger pointed at me, he spat, "I already told that bitch to get off my property. You are not welcome either."

Nash spoke in an eerily calm fashion. "We have

a few questions for you and then we will leave. Loose the attitude. It will not get you anywhere but a hospital bed. I'm itching to put you six feet under for pulling a shotgun on Ms. Briggs."

His body sagged with the loss of a fight looming but his beady eyes squinted with barely controlled rage.

We stayed rooted to our spots as Nash started the questioning. "Do you know what happened to your daughter?"

"I've already told that cunt that I don't have a daughter." Spittle flew out of his mouth.

"Again, I will ask you to refrain from addressing Ms. Briggs in a hostile way." With his feet shoulder width apart and his hands relaxed at his sides he continued. "We know that Gray is your daughter, Mr. McCullum. Why is it that you deny that she is?"

Harold threw his hands up in the air and blew out a breath. His body sagged as though the weight of the world hung on his shoulders. "My wife had an affair shortly after we had gotten married. The son-of-a-bitch who she cheated with got her pregnant. Gray is not mine and she will never be." He spat the words with disgust.

I drew in a breath, ready to ask a question, when Nash stopped me with a deadly glare. This was his rodeo and I was to keep my mouth shut. He was here to get answers.

"Why not divorce your wife, disowning them completely?"

"Because she is my wife and I own her."

I gritted my teeth hard enough that the muscles in my jaw began to ache. I itched to throat punch him and then knee him in his cowardly balls.

"Do you know where Gray might be or how she might have disappeared?"

"I don't know and I don't care either."

"She was just an innocent child, you monster. She doesn't deserve what happened to her. She was loved and the child of your wife, for God's sake. Don't you have any compassion at all?" I spewed.

"My *wife*——" he drawled out, "made her choices. Now she has to live with the consequences. Now, if you'll excuse me, I have to get to work."

"One more thing," Nash calmly said. "If you lay a hand on your wife and I find out, you're a dead man and you can guarantee that no one will find your body."

"Are you threatening me?"

"Nope, just making a statement. Oh, and when we find Gray, you better hope to fucking God that she is still alive and unharmed." He turned toward me. "Let's go."

I grinned from ear to ear as I took one last look at Harold. *Take that, you nasty little slime ball!* Nash had connections in dark places and disposing of Harold would be an easy task. Not that I wanted him to knowingly put himself in danger but ridding the world of the likes of Harold would not hurt my feelings in the least.

I looked out the side window. "You were a little scary back there."

He placed his hand gently on my thigh. "Are you scared of me?"

I chanced a look at him and he was a beautiful sight. I could get lost in his eyes alone. His strong and chiseled features made me feel safe and at home. *Was I scared of him?* That was the easiest answer of all: yes, but only frightened that he would break my heart. So, I lied to him. "No."

He nodded and placed his hand back on the wheel as though I had burned him. "He doesn't know where Gray is. I do believe that he is grateful that she is gone."

"Why didn't you demand more answers? You could've gotten them." I was suddenly angry with him for not pressuring Harold more.

"His body language told me enough. I don't need to know about his shitty marriage or what goes on behind closed doors. That's between them. I could see the scared look in his eyes when I asked him if he knew where Gray was. He wasn't worried about me learning any deep secret, only that of his safety."

"But he was so angry. Doesn't that tell you that he might be hiding something?" I flipped my hands in the air with exasperation.

"No. He was pissed because I called him out on abusing his wife and knowing that it wouldn't take much for me to extinguish his life."

"Aren't you afraid that he will take it out on Penny? I have to warn her."

"He won't and you will do no such thing. Penny is our key to unlocking everything. She is the one with all of the secrets. Harold doesn't know his wife as well as he thought he did."

I sat there and mulled over his statement for the rest of the drive. *Was I looking at this case all wrong?* I had pinned all of my hopes of solving the case on Harold. I hadn't taken in to consideration Penny's motives at all. I kept seeing her as the victim. She was in many ways but could she have done something to Gray? I couldn't wrap my brain around that. She projected an all-consuming love for her daughter. *Was it possible that she physically harmed her own child? Why wait until she was close to being an adult? If she wanted her daughter out of the way, wouldn't she have disposed of her long before now?* Nothing in this case made any damn sense.

Nash parked the car in the office lot. He turned toward me. "Skye, you are getting close to the answers. I can feel it."

His hope did nothing to improve my spirits. "I hope you're right, Nash. Right now, I don't feel that way."

"I've cleared my schedule for next week. I had Lisa book our itinerary. We leave first thing Monday morning. I'll have her book our return as soon as we have some answers."

"What if it's a bust? How long do you think it will take? I don't want you to have to babysit me, Nash. I'm a big girl and can do this on my own."

"I know you can handle this on your own but if it's all right with you, I need to make sure that you are safe. Being hundreds of miles away is not a comforting thought if you need my help."

"Would you do the same for Ryker or Hawke?"

His blank expression told me more than I wanted to know. "Nash, I'm going by myself. You trusted me to do my job and I will. Without you holding my hand through the process."

He opened his mouth to interrupt, but I held my hand up to stop him.

"I appreciate it. I really do, but how am I ever

going to prove myself as a respected team member if you continue to coddle me in front of the guys? I'll be honest with you, I'm nervous about flying down there and snooping around and you're not right around the corner to bail me out. But, you know what? If I don't do this on my own, then I will never know how good of an asset I truly am for the company."

His jaw muscles worked frantically. He was pissed but he also knew that I was right.

"Okay, Briggs."

I winced as soon as my last name crossed his lips. He was back in boss mode. I hated that I lost what little camaraderie we had built.

I had to do this on my own. His feelings for me would cloud my vision and undercut my confidence in solving the case. If I allowed him to travel with me, he would inadvertently take over the case to make sure that I was out of danger. It was in his nature to protect at all costs and in turn, it would rob me of an immeasurable gain of experience.

CHAPTER 15

"**N**ASH KISSED ME. WELL, KISSED a trail down my neck."

I wasn't finished but Jackie wasn't concerned with my ending of the story before she rudely interrupted me.

"Oh, my word! Is his dick as big as I imagine it to be? I bet he knows how to please a woman, like multiple times."

Her excitement had me belly laughing so hard that a lone tear slid down my cheek.

"If you would've let me finish, then you would know that it never went that far. He broke away before anything could happen. I swear to God that in those few precious minutes, he had me begging for more."

"What stopped him? I mean, come on, you're a hottie."

"I wouldn't go that far. I don't know. I'm pretty sure that he freaked out a little and we were going to go interview Gray's dad. Plus, I am his employee. We can't afford to mix business with pleasure. You know as well as I do that those relationships never work out."

"Then go screw like rabbits and you open up your own firm."

"I love your thinking but I'm not experienced enough to go out on my own."

"Who says?"

"I do. Nash dominates the PI field and rightfully so. If you want the best, you hire him."

"So what you are saying is that he got you all worked up, left you high and dry, and you're not going to demand more?"

"Basically. And I like Omar. He is available."

"That sounds like you are settling."

"Not really. Omar is just as delicious but in a more accessible way. Why keep fighting a losing battle with Nash, when I can have a real shot with Omar?"

"Girl, I can't keep up with you but I support whatever decision you make. And why am I just now hearing about this Omar guy?"

I recounted everything about Omar that I could to bring her up to speed.

"Because we haven't talked in a couple of days. Anyhoo, did you score that decorating job?"

"Sure did. They hired me on the spot!"

"That's awesome. I am so happy for you."

"Thanks, girl. This is my biggest project yet and could solidify my career. I've already started. If everything goes according to plan, the job should be done in a couple of weeks. I hate to cut this short but I got to get back to work. I've been working late nights to get the job done quicker."

She couldn't see my smile but I was genuinely excited for her. "Make sure you don't burn yourself out."

"I won't. There is no sense lying awake at night worrying about making it perfect when I can utilize my time by working my ass off while the house is empty."

"All right, sister. Call me when you can. Can I see it when you're finished?"

"Absolutely! Later, babe."

"Later."

Some days, talking with her over the phone made me miss her company more. I needed a good bitch session but that would have to wait until she finished this project.

I popped in a microwavable dinner and grabbed my notebook. My mind whirled with unanswered questions. I was banking on the sister giving me a lead. It might be possible that she might provide all the answers. I highly doubted it. It was wishful thinking at best.

Lisa sent me my itinerary this afternoon. I noticed that there was no return date. Nash must want me to stay in Florida until I deemed it necessary to come back. *Shit, what about the other caseloads I had going?*

"Donovan." Nash answered on the first ring.

I sighed. He had closed himself off from me. I could tell in the coldness of his voice. I hoped that I hadn't caused irreparable damage to our friendship.

"Hey, boss. What would you like me to do with my other cases? I only have a couple of cheaters to scout out. They came across my desk the other day."

"They can wait. Call your clients tomorrow and let them know that you will be out of town. If they are unwilling to wait for your return, then give me those clients and I will take care of it."

"Are you sure, Nash? You are busy enough without adding my stuff too."

"I told you that I would take care of it and I will."

"Look, I don't know what crawled up your ass but I'm tired of receiving the shit end of it. I'm sorry about the other morning. There was a line crossed and Scout's

honor——I won't cross it again. I'm also sorry for pissing you off by wanting to go alone to Florida."

"Are you done?"

"Yep." My lips made a popping sound.

"I'm having a hard time reining in my attraction for you. I'm not sorry about kissing you. Hell, I wanted to do more. Going to Florida alone was the right call. It will give us both a chance to clear our heads. I also understand your need for the guys to respect you and I'll tell you this, that we all respect the hell out of you. You have already proved yourself as a valuable team member. Utilize this time away to focus on the case and nothing but the case."

"What happens when I come back? Do you want me to quit? What are you saying?"Anxiety spread through my body. I didn't want to quit working for him and I certainly didn't want it to be awkward at work.

"We go back to the way things were as though nothing happened. I don't want you to quit and I'm not firing you."

What was I supposed to say to that? It would be impossible to forget the feelings that he invoked. The soft and yet demanding way his lips traveled the length of my sensitive skin. I shivered with the memory. "If you can forget, then so can I. I'll check in with you once I get settled."

"Talk with you soon."

"Bye."

That conversation sucked worse than when the dentist pulled my wisdom teeth. I would gladly remove the rest of my teeth than feel the cracks he had just pounded into my heart. Florida was looking better and better.

I picked up my phone after I heard the text chime.

You busy tomorrow night?

My grin came easy enough but it wasn't the wattage that I had wanted to feel when I saw Omar's name across my screen. Damn Nash for screwing that up. *Was I up for company?* I debated for a couple of seconds. *Sure. Why not?*

Nope, what did you have in mind?

How about dinner at my place and some Netflix?

Sounds great. The new Beauty and the Beast is on.

Umm, if that's what you want.

I laughed heartily out loud. I'm not a big emoji person but I picked the one with the winking eye and the tongue sticking out.

LOL. I'm kidding. You can pick the movie and make dinner.

You are not funny at all! Pasta and the Sound of Music?

You're on!

See you at six.

It's a date.

The Sound of Music was a good movie and I

would be down with watching it again. Even though he was probably joking, I bet I could get him to watch it. Mental torture was a fun game!

CHAPTER 16

I GOT UP EARLY AND HEADED to my mom's for breakfast. Every Saturday, she made pancakes, sausage, and eggs. When I could, I showed up. Her pancakes were to die for. She made them from scratch and no restaurant had even come close. I was about to indulge in a carb overload catatonic state.

"These are so good," I mumbled around a mouthful.

"You want some more?"

I nodded because I was still shoveling in the last bite on my plate. She piled more onto my plate. I wouldn't be able to eat all of them, but I would sure as hell put a dent in them.

"How's work?" Dad sat back in his chair and rubbed his bloated belly.

"Good. I'm heading out Monday to Florida to interview the aunt of the girl who had gone missing."

"How long are you going to be gone?" he asked, surprised that I was leaving the state. All of my cases prior to this one had never required it.

"I'm not sure. It's open-ended at this moment. It all depends on what the aunt has to say. I'm thinking a couple of days, tops. I might go to the beach and take a day or two to tour the area."

"You deserve a mini-vacation," Mom commented.

Yes––yes, I did.

"How was the painting class?"

Her face lit up like a Christmas tree. "It was a ton of fun. I'll show you what I painted, before you leave."

"She called me, drunker than a skunk off that wine. She couldn't drive herself home."

"Lee! I was not drunk."

My dad and I both snorted at her mock outrage. My mother loved her wine just as much as I did. It was no surprise that she got tipsy. They don't serve enough wine at those things to be falling down wasted but after a glass or two, she wouldn't consider getting behind the wheel. For which I am extremely thankful for. I spent the rest of the morning and the afternoon soaking up their company. It had been awhile since I had more than a couple of hours catching up with them.

I had programmed Omar's address into my Waze app on my phone. He lived about fifteen minutes from me so I pulled into his drive in no time. I got out of the car and admired his cute bungalow. The yard was immaculately kept, unlike mine. For a bachelor, I was already impressed. I hoped the inside wasn't a complete bachelor pad but at the same time I didn't really care either way. I was curious as to what the inside said about him. I started up the porch steps and looked longingly at the outdoor furniture. The wooden Adirondack chairs had thick cushions that I could imagine sinking into with a cup of steaming coffee. That would be an incredible place for a nightcap and a good spot for people watching. His neighborhood seemed to be one where kids played in the front yard and couples took nightly strolls, hand-in-hand.

I knocked on the blue painted door. He opened up the door, looking delicious in his worn jeans and soft cotton gray shirt. I wondered whether the material was as velvety to the touch as it was pleasing to my eyes.

"My eyes are up here." His boyish grin made him look even younger than he was.

"They aren't as pretty as your shirt. May I?" I raised my hand to touch the material.

"You won't hear any objections from me."

I rubbed my hand down from his chest to the waistline of his jeans. The cotton was wonderfully silky, which contradicted the hard muscled torso underneath.

"If you keep that up, dinner will have to be postponed." His mouth formed a generous smile but his eyes simmered with heated desire.

"I'm too hungry to let your wonderful meal suffer. It smells delicious and I'm still standing outside."

He swung the door open wider. "After you."

I walked through the door and into the small foyer. An entry table hugged the far right wall. Its rich mahogany was covered with his keys and work-issued belt.

"Would you like a drink? The pasta is done and

I only need to throw the garlic bread in and then we can get you fed."

"I would love a glass of wine, if you have it."

"I picked up two bottles today. You have a choice of sweet red or white. I don't know if either of them are any good. I don't drink the stuff. I'm a beer man. It's what the lady at the store recommended."

I chuckled. "I'd love a glass of the red, thank you."

"Coming right up. If you'd like, you can go out the kitchen door and on to the patio. It's a perfect night to eat outside. I'll bring your glass out."

"Sounds great. Do you need any help before I head out there?"

"Nope, I've got it all under control."

His home was spacious with the open floor plan. The living room, kitchen, and dining room were one large room. He had an enormous flat-screen TV with a black-leather sectional. I bet the seats reclined too. The kitchen was spacious, with an island in the middle. Everything looked lived in but not dirty. He kept a clean house; at least, today it was. He had a good eye on decorating. It was better than what my house looked like before Jackie got a hold of it.

His yard was maybe a half an acre and again, immaculately kept. The patio had a covered roof with two ceiling fans. The table was from a high-end store. This man had expensive taste. The space would be great for entertaining. He even had an outdoor couch set off to the corner with a fireplace table. *Roasted marshmallows—yes, please.*

He emerged from the sliding glass doors with a

chilled glass of red in one hand and a Coors Light in the other. He handed me the glass and sat in the chair next to me.

"Thank you."

"Don't thank me until you've tried it."

I took a small sip and declared it pretty decent. "It's not bad. You did good."

"Thank God. Now, if you like the meal, then we should be on solid ground."

I chuckled. "I'm a sucker for a man who can cook."

"It's a good thing that my mama taught me how."

"Do you have a large family?"

His smile showed me the love he had for his family. "I have three older brothers and two younger sisters."

"Wow. It must be crazy around the holidays! I am an only child." I took a breath. "What's it like having siblings? Do you all get along?"

"It's like a crazy, loud, and fun circus. Everyone shouts over one another when they talk. When we were little, my brothers and I fought like cats and dogs but we are as tight as they come now. My sisters are a pain in my ass but I love them to death."

"What do they all do?"

"My brothers and I all followed in my dad's footsteps into law enforcement. My one sister is in college to become a pediatrician and the youngest one is about to graduate from high school." He took a drink of his beer. "What was it like being an only child?"

"It was great because I had all of my parents'

attention and yet it sucked because I had all of their attention. They are mine, so I love them."

"When I was younger, I wished to be an only child but I wouldn't change our household for anything. My siblings, as well as my parents, are my biggest supporters. I couldn't imagine them not being in my life."

"Mine too. I've got plenty of friends who fit that bill too. We are equally lucky to have such loving families."

"Yes we are." He set his beer down. "Are you ready to eat?"

"Starving."

"Good. Let's go dish up!"

"Lead the way, Master Chef."

"That has a nice ring to it."

"Then let's hope you live up to that title."

His laughter was rich and settled deep into my bones. He was fun to be around. My nerves had settled and it felt as though we had known each other forever. I envied his self-confidence; he was gorgeous, but didn't boast about it. He was actually quite humble. His sarcasm flowed as naturally as mine and he made me feel at home in his presence. That was on top of his good looks and smoking-hot body. *What more could a girl ask for?* I couldn't think of a damn thing. I had hit the man lottery with this one. I hoped my lucky streak continued and he didn't turn out to be a shithead.

Dinner was superb, as good as any five-star restaurant.

"My compliments to the chef. Outstanding!"

His eyes lit up with excitement. "I'm glad you

approve."

"Definitely. Can you cook for me every night?"

"I'll cook for you anytime you want. If that's every night, I'll thank my lucky stars to have such wonderful company."

"Just wonderful?" Yeah, it was juvenile but I fished for more compliments.

"Will funny work?"

I squinted, mock anger in my attitude.

His deep laughter rang out. "How about sexy, charming, and sexy."

I laughed. "You already said sexy."

"Adoringly sexy."

I scrunched up my face.

"So sexy that I would love nothing more than to throw you on this table and have you for dessert."

My mouth opened in shock. *Damn if that wasn't the best compliment that I have ever heard.*

"Too much?"

I smiled wickedly. "Just right. How about I help you clean up and then we take our drinks to the front porch so that I can acquaint myself with those beautiful Adirondack chairs that have been calling my name since I got here."

"I prefer dessert but your suggestion sounds pretty good too."

With the two of us combining our efforts, everything was cleaned and put away in record time. I followed him out the door. He made a right instead of a left toward the chairs.

He motioned for me to join him on the glider. "Come here."

Oh, even better. I didn't see that when I first got here. I gladly sat next to him. He put his arm around my shoulders and pulled me against him. The night had chilled but his body heat kept me plenty warm.

"I love this weather and your porch––" I looked up at him, prepared to thank him for such a wonderful evening but his lips promptly smothered my last words.

He moved his lips expertly over mine, silently demanding more with each kiss. Each time his tongue explored the recesses of my mouth, a shiver of desire raced through me. My hand roamed over his solid chest, over his shoulder, and to the back of his neck. My fingers threaded through the silky feel of his short hair. I fisted my hand, bringing the short strands tightly around my fingers. I swallowed his guttural moan as I pulled him tighter against me.

Our kissing could've lasted for hours or seconds. I had no way of knowing. I only cared because he placed one sweet kiss on my forehead as he lifted his head away. I wanted more but how much more did I really want? For being a grown ass woman, I was acting timid. My heart wanted another man even as my body responded to Omar. All three parts of me were at war. My brain shouted for me to try a relationship with him. He was a good man. My heart panged with guilt at the thought of having sex with someone other than Nash. My vagina told the other two to shut up; it was her turn and she wanted Omar––Nash be damned. I almost giggled at the thought of my vagina as a whore. She didn't care which one pleasured her at the moment. All she wanted was the release of pure ecstasy. Ultimately, I was more than relieved that he had pulled away.

I remained curled into him for some time before I said anything. "I had a wonderful time tonight," I said truthfully.

The spark of desire remained checked but I could see traces of it as I gazed into his beautiful eyes. One word and we could be upstairs and feeling equally satiated. I hated to feel like a prude but the humor that replaced his desire let me off the hook.

"I did too. How about dinner tomorrow? Same time, same place."

His irresistibly devastating grin had turned my insides into a knotted ball. I enjoyed his company and the way that he made me feel. If we took this slow, it could work. The chemistry was there, the conversation was comfortable, and he could cook.

"Sounds great. I've got another session with Ryker tomorrow so I may be a couple of minutes late. If that is okay with you?"

"Perfect. I'll make sure it's ready about the time you get here so that we can refuel your body."

His devilish grin implied the type of refueling I just might need.

I laughed nervously then gave him a peck on the cheek as I walked to my car.

"Good-night, Skye."

"See you tomorrow."

CHAPTER 17

"YOU KNOW I HATE YOU right now!" I panted.

Ryker's laughter echoed off the gym walls. "You'll be thanking me later if you ever have to use the moves I've taught you."

"Maybe, but do you have to be so fucking rough about it?"

I winced as my tired muscles started to cramp and a bead of sweat dropped into my eye. I used the collar of my shirt to rub frantically at my lid, trying to eradicate the burning sensation. That should be a new form of torture; dripping sweat into the eyeballs of your enemy. They would surrender within a matter of seconds, guaranteed.

"Your attacker will not go easy on you and neither will I. So quit being a baby, lick your wounds, and take a hot shower."

I stuck my tongue out at him. *Childish?* Absolutely, but the deep laughter that burst out of him made it all worth it.

"Go home, Briggs, and be careful in Florida."

I raised my eyebrows in shock. "You worried about me, Ryker?"

"Nope. I know you can handle it." He winked.

I chuckled. *He cared.* "Let's hope so." I mumbled

so that he couldn't hear the tiny bit of doubt that wiggled its way into my mind.

I didn't have time to soak in a hot tub and erase the tenderness of my muscles. I did use the pulsating showerhead to ease them to the point that I could move my tired body without wincing. I put on some comfy leggings and a thigh-length sweater dress. The nights were getting cooler as winter approached. I hated the long winter months but the first fall of snow almost made the brittle temperatures worth it. I slipped on my fur-lined leopard print Crocks and headed out the door.

I had packed for my trip before my lesson with Ryker. That way I would feel freer to relax and enjoy Omar's company. I wouldn't have to worry about accomplishing that small feat when I got home. I had to be at the airport by ten in the morning, so I could sleep in a bit. Bless Lisa for recognizing the fact that I needed an extra few winks before spending the rest of my day cooped up with travel plans. Flying wasn't an issue; it was the lag time in the airport that sucked. There were only so many bookstores that I could peruse before they all looked the same. Let's face it: those newsstands basically publicized all of the same material. I put my iPad in my carry-on bag so I could get lost in one of many steamy romances that I had downloaded this morning. With my return date open-ended, I needed plenty of reading material for possible beach time.

I pulled into his drive and put the car in park. I grabbed my purse and headed up the narrow walk to his front door. This time, I didn't have to knock. He probably saw my headlights pull in.

"Good evening, gorgeous." His voice held a rasp of excitement.

"Good evening, to you too." An easy smile played at the corners of my mouth.

As usual, he was mouth-watering in his worn denim jeans and molded cotton shirt. He held out his hand as I got closer. I gently placed mine in his. He pulled me tight against his body and pressed his lips to mine, caressing my mouth more than kissing it. His soft mouth was exactly the hello I was looking for.

He pulled away, but kept his warm eyes locked on mine. "Are you hungry?"

"I'm starved."

"Good. Come on in and we will eat."

We both filled our plates with lasagna and garlic bread. The smell alone tortured my famished belly.

"I know we had pasta last night but lasagna was the easiest."

"I don't cook much for myself so anything you make is better than a frozen meal."

"How was your workout with Ryker?"

"Excruciating."

"That bad?"

I took another bite before I answered. *God, this was like pouring heaven straight onto my taste buds.*

"I have to say that if this whole cop career isn't working out, you would make an excellent chef." My smile was genuine. I sighed. "Ryker doesn't hold back. He is strong and makes it tough to break his holds. He tossed me around like a ragdoll. After it's all said and done, it's worth it. My muscles are screaming profanities at me right now, but your cooking is helping."

"Is he teaching you strictly self-defense moves?"

"Mostly. He digs deeper and takes on the role of an enemy to a whole new level. I asked him to train me because I thought that he would be the easier choice of the three of them. I haven't had the pleasure of working with Hawke, but between Ryker and Nash, Ryker is the more evil. I think that Nash takes it easy on me."

"Maybe so, but I think that learning from all three will give you the ultimate advantage. I could teach you some moves too." His voice was laced with innuendos.

"I might surprise you with some of my own." My voice dipped seductively.

Heat pooled in his creamy coffee-colored eyes. "I bet you could and I am looking forward to them."

My uncertainty from the other night had not reared its ugly head. Tonight my mind was in sync with my body.

I winked and took our empty plates to the sink. "You want some help cleaning this up?"

"Leave them. They can wait." He scooted his chair back and walked forward, stopping right in front of me.

My hips touched the counter. I had nowhere to go, and I didn't want to. I wanted his mouth and his hands to explore every inch of me.

I leaned lightly into him and tilted my face toward his. I parted my lips as I raised myself to meet his kiss. He pressed his lips against mine and gently covered my mouth. His lips and tongue explored mine as though he had all the time in the world. It was a sweet and torturous seduction.

In one fell swoop his mouth left mine and he scooped me up, practically running up the stairs to what I hoped was his bedroom. I wouldn't mind the counter, kitchen table, couch, but a bed had a hell of a lot more room to do all of the things that I wanted him to do to me.

He carried me through the bedroom door and I gently placed my feet on the carpeted floor. In about two seconds I was about to show him how non-fragile I was. We both had on entirely too many clothes. I wasn't beyond stripping and getting to the good part. My patience was next to nil when it came to foreplay. I stood before him and reached out to grab hold of his shirt. I wanted to see more of his perfectly sculpted body. His form-fitted shirt didn't leave much to the imagination; however, I wanted to run my hands and mouth over every peak and valley of his toned body.

He halted my hands before they reached the silky material. "Patience. We have all night."

No we didn't. This wasn't a sleepover. Orgasm and leave––that was my plan.

I went for his shirt again. "I have a plane to catch tomorrow morning. You are not allowed to keep me up half the night."

A wicked smile from him sent shivers of desire down my spine.

"Ms. Briggs, you have so much to learn. Have you ever been with a Latin lover?"

"No. Is that supposed to mean something?" I crossed my hands under my breasts.

Desire danced in his eyes. "I won't explain it to

you. You'll just have to trust me to show you."

He placed my hands to my sides and with practiced patience, lifted my sweater inch by tantalizing inch until he slid the thick material over my head. He soaked in every inch of skin he exposed. I wanted to squirm under his gaze, but I held still as he undressed me. My nipples beaded tightly, pleading with him to touch them. With a featherlight touch, his fingertips grazed my quivering stomach, down to the waistband of my leggings. He slid his deft fingers under the material of my pants and underwear. He curled his fingers, grabbing a hold of both pieces of clothing and moved them over my thighs and down my legs.

I was completely bare and withering with need. My core was drenched and he barely touched me. He walked me backward until the back of my legs made contact with the side of the bed. His strong hands went gently around my waist, picking me up as though I weighed nothing, and laid me upon the bed. As he hovered over my body, instead of brown eyes, the color of storm clouds gazed back at me. I smiled wickedly as those gray eyes scanned every inch of my bare skin.

"You are perfection, *mi hermosa reina*."

The words of his native language rolled off his tongue seductively. They made me hotter, which I didn't think was possible. I didn't have a clue as to what he said and I didn't care. His words also brought me into the present and the man who I had begun to fantasize about was not the one seducing me. I hated myself for comparing the two of them. It wasn't fair to Omar to think of

Nash when he was the one making me feel so desired.

I bit my lower lip and watched him stand. All thoughts of Nash disappeared as I raised my eyes and watched as he removed his shirt. The hardness of his body looked as though it were carved from marble. I licked my lips with heady anticipation. His dark eyes never left mine as he climbed back on to the bed and hovered over my body. He lowered his mouth and captured mine. He took his time kissing me until my toes curled. His soft lips kissed their way down my neck and to the valley between my breasts. I inhaled as my blood scorched my veins. My breasts were heavy and the hard peaks begged for his attention. He continued to whisper words of his first language and I was lost. Lost in his touch and tantalizing voice. All the while, his mouth and tongue sent delicious shivers along my skin.

His tongue slid over the tight bud, creating an electric zinging sensation all the way to my core. I arched my back with each sting of his bite. When he moved to my other breast, I thought for sure that I was going to have an orgasm. His mouth played my body like a finely tuned instrument. I was at his mercy. A breathy moan worked its way out with every sweet swipe of his tongue as he soothed the sting of his teeth. My fists clung to the sheets to keep me grounded. He continued his passionate trek over my ribs and down my quivering stomach.

He placed tiny kisses along my hipbones, inching his way between my trembling thighs. I couldn't keep them together anymore. They fell away as soon as his skilled tongue licked along my wet folds. I opened wider as his hands cupped my ass and he molded my pussy to his mouth. I purred, basking in every stimulating sensation that was bringing me closer to the brink of having an outer-body experience.

He continued his feast until my entire body had splintered into millions of tiny pieces. I fought unconsciousness during the brief moment it took him to shed the remainder of his clothes. He positioned himself between my legs, teasing my entrance with the tip of his cock. I wanted more. Scratch that—I craved him to fill my body completely.

"Please, Omar," I begged.

"Patience, *mi reina*."

"What does that mean?"

Instead of answering me, he lowered his mouth to my ear and whispered the words again as he pushed himself inside me.

"Ah, more," I pleaded. I wrapped my legs around his beautifully sculpted ass and drew him in tighter.

"Skye." His husky voice sounded as though it pained him to go slow.

"Harder."

I wanted him to take what he wanted. I opened freely for him and I'd be damned if I could stop him. He felt exquisite. He had stretched and filled me to the hilt. I felt him everywhere. His hands roamed, touching my breasts, and his mouth licked and bit along my sensitive neck. All the while, his hips kept thrusting. It was almost too much for me to handle. My body felt as though it were coming apart at the seams. My inner muscles tightened with my impending orgasm.

He pulled my arms above my head. With one hand, he held them prisoner. His other hand moved between our bodies. His thumb stroked my pulsating clit. "Look at me," he commanded.

I opened my lids and the heat that blazed back at me shattered my existence. I screamed out his name as my orgasm ripped through me. His thrusts increased and brought around the most exquisite torture as my inner walls clenched around him. He tilted his head back, groaning with his own release.

He gazed into my eyes with a well-satisfied look. "You are exquisite." He pulled away from me and disposed of the condom.

I burrowed under the covers to wait for his return. *What the fuck was I doing?* I should go home, but when he came back to bed and pulled my back to his front, I let his strong arms lull me to sleep instead.

The smell of morning breakfast drifted through my nose, beckoning me awake. I lazily stretched my tired muscles. I smiled, giddy at the thought of what had transpired last night. He was an exceptional lover, the best I had ever had. There was no going back to my battery-operated toys. They would never compare to last night. I would have loved a repeat of last night but I was starving and whatever he was making downstairs made my mouth water. I took a peek at my watch. It was only seven. I had plenty of time to eat and get home before I had to leave for the airport. A moment of sadness entered my thoughts at having to go without Omar and his magical bedroom skills for a couple of days. I quickly shrugged the feeling off and put on my clothes from last night.

I entered the kitchen as Omar dished up breakfast.

"Smells delicious."

He turned toward me and an easy smile played at the corners of his mouth. "Just some eggs and bacon with a little avocado and salsa. I hope you like avocado."

"Sure do. I'm not a picky eater."

"I wanted to make sure that you were well fed before you went to the airport. I wasn't sure what time you flew out so I decided to make breakfast instead of ravishing you." He winked.

"Your cooking is way better." I coughed into my hand, trying to mask my laughter from the inner fire that ignited in his eyes.

He stalked toward me and grabbed my sweater, pulling me into his hard body. "You'll pay for that."

My eyebrows raised a fraction in silent challenge. *Fuck breakfast.* I wanted him more.

His lips crashed down upon mine. It was pure savagery. Our hands were everywhere. He twisted me around so that my back was to him. His strong hands brushed over my breasts and my back arched. He walked us toward the kitchen table. He bent me over when my hips came in contact with the hardwood. He ran his hand along my back and lifted my sweater up. His hand caressed my ass, bringing more moisture to my core. He removed his hands and I whimpered at the loss. In a swift motion, he yanked my pants and underwear down. My inner walls clenched with the need for him.

"So beautiful. Are you ready for me, *mi reina*?" His voice was throaty.

"Yes," I moaned breathlessly.

I gripped the sides of the table as he spread my legs wider. With a quick thrust, he filled me all the way. He didn't hold back this time. He took me with a vengeance and I begged for more. His cock was pumping fast and furiously, and I loved every inch of it. He reached his finger around to my clit. With one swipe of his finger, I clenched around his thick shaft. I screamed his name as the world became dark and I saw stars. After a couple of more thrusts, he had moaned his own release. He pulled out and kissed the small of my back.

"Am I forgiven for this morning?" His voice was laced with sarcasm.

"Mmm, hmm."

Before I could stand and collect myself, he pulled my pants up and brought me to face him. He kissed me slowly, which I melted into.

"Let's eat."

"Typical––only thinking of food." I winked and grabbed my plate as my belly growled.

He threw his head back with laughter. "I can't win, can I?"

"Nope. No sense in trying."

In a split second, all of his playfulness took on a sickening look.

"What's the matter? Are you okay?" My voice was laced with concern.

One minute, we were laughing and then the next, he looked as though he were about to vomit.

"I got so carried away that I forgot to put a condom on. Shit! I can't believe how stupid I was." His hand flew to his hair and grabbed at the silky strands.

I placed a kiss on his cheek. "I'm clean and on birth control. I guess I should ask you if you're clean?"

His audible sigh ricocheted loudly off the tiled walls of the kitchen. "I'm clean. I never forget to wear one."

I secretly enjoyed his concern and the fact that he had gotten so carried away that he forgot. *Hello, I am in my late thirties; this isn't my first rodeo.* "It's all good. Can we eat now?" I laughed. "I'm on borrowed time."

His chuckle was more reserved this time around. "Yep. When are you coming back?"

I paused before I shoveled in a forkful of food. "I don't know. I'm heading out to Florida to interview the aunt of the girl who went missing. I'm hoping only a couple of days, tops."

In between bites, he said, "Why would it take you a couple of days to interview the family member? Shouldn't it take a day, tops?"

"I'm thinking about taking a day or two for a mini-vacation. Sit on the beach and enjoy the warmer weather."

"Want some company? I might be able to meet you out there."

"Seriously?" I stammered in bewilderment.

He shrugged nonchalantly. "Why not? You, the beach, and marathon sex—what's not to like about that?"

A wave of apprehension swept through me.

This whole scene was moving a little fast for me. I needed some time to think about him meeting up with me. We had only gone out a couple of times.

"How about I call you when I get down there before I give you a solid answer?"

The smile that he gave me never reached his eyes. "Sounds good. Let me know a day or two ahead if you can so I can give my boss adequate notice."

I nodded. That was fair. We finished our breakfast with minor tension crackling in the air. I hated that my insecurities put a damper on a wonderful morning. I put my dishes in the sink and picked up my purse.

"Thank you for a wonderful time. I'll give you a call when I land."

He seared my lips with a kiss that I wouldn't soon forget. "Be safe and I look forward to your call."

I nodded once again because what more needed to be said? I had to get going if I were going to make my flight. There was no need to prolong this good-bye and I got the feeling that I had disappointed him. I liked the thought of him joining me but then again I also wanted the time to myself. I hoped that he would still be here if I decided to tell him no. I shook my thoughts away. I didn't have to answer him for another day or so. I needed to get down there and track down the aunt. My love life was not important at the moment.

CHAPTER 18

I RACED TO THE AIRPORT AS though the devil were on my heels. I would be pushing it to make my flight once I got through security. I wore flats so I could easily take off my shoes. No jewelry or belts, just some yoga pants and a long-sleeved shirt. It was chilly here but once I stepped out of the Jacksonville airport, it would be warm and humid. At least that was what my weather app had told me.

I breezed through security and found a seat close to the gate. I had twenty minutes to spare. I breathed out a sigh of relief as I sat down. I was already sore from last night and this morning's sexcapades. It was a gratifying feeling while I was sitting down but running through the terminal was a tad bit uncomfortable. Instead of powering up my iPad, I decided to people watch instead.

Airports always reminded me of an ant colony. Every person tittered here and there, with specific tasks on their mind. It was an organized type of chaos. Normally, I kept my nose in a book and ignored everything around me. However, today, I felt compelled to watch. There were kids running and laughing and their parents had annoyed looks on their faces. Most of the people around me were reading a paper, magazine, munching on snacks, and oblivious of their surroundings. It baffled my mind the way that we as a society could happily ignore most of the population surrounding us. I didn't understand it and yet I also reacted the same way. I didn't go out of my way to communicate to a stranger. I sat in my seat, observing from the outside.

The row that I was assigned was called to stand in line. I waited as patiently as I could until it was my turn to have my ticket scanned. I stepped on the plane and quickly found an open window seat in the back of the plane. I was in no hurry to be the first off, only to stand at baggage claim and wait for my bags. Jack always said that no one liked to sit in the back of the plane and it was the best place to snag a window seat. Everyone would vie for the front, so just head straight back. So I took her advice and sat in the back. Plus, it gave the ground crew time to unload the luggage and the lag time from debarking to picking up your luggage was considerably less.

Our flight time was relatively short, but long enough for me to catch a quick nap. I wiped the crusted drool off the corner of my lip before I gathered my stuff. I disembarked and took the long trek toward baggage. I was digging this airport; it was small and easy to navigate.

In no time at all, I was in my rental, blasting the air conditioning. I would've never thought that Florida would be this hot at this time of the year. Holy, hell the humidity had backhanded me hard right across my face when I stepped out of the cool airport. Even Indiana's hottest summer day couldn't compare to the swampy mugginess of this state. I hoped that the beach felt better than this. Otherwise, I wouldn't be staying long—in and out. I pushed the gas pedal farther down when I could feel the bead of sweat traveling a path down between my breasts. *Shit, how do people live in this kind of heat?* It was suffocating. I had the air running on full blast and I still felt just as sticky as when I started the car.

In my mind, Florida was nothing but sand, beaches, and palm trees. From what I'd seen, this part of the state was saturated with pine trees. They weren't as pretty as the thick blue spruces back home. These were tall and scraggily looking. It was as though someone had ripped the limbs of the pine from halfway down and only left the top needles.

I crossed the bridge going into Fernandina Beach, following the directions from my phone app to the hotel. I followed the roundabout and pulled into the sand-covered parking lot. Now *this* was what Florida was supposed to look like. I could see the beach from the parking lot. The smell of salt and the crashing of the waves automatically put my mind and body at ease. Every inch of my skin itched to be on the beach. I checked in as quickly as the front desk allowed. I practically ran to the elevators and to my room. I wanted out of these travel clothes and my bathing suit on.

I sat on the perfectly made king-sized bed and dialed Nash. I bounced a little as I waited for him to pick up. This was nice and firm and making me long for a good night's sleep.

"Did you find the hotel easy enough?" His tone

was brusque and business-like.

I sighed. It was as it should be. "Sure did. Everything has been relatively straightforward. Easiest first trip I've ever been on by myself. I didn't screw anything up and didn't get lost."

I was proud of myself for that. Hell, the only place I've ever been was Indiana.

"You've never been anywhere but Indiana?"

I could hear the surprise in his voice.

"Nope. When I was growing up, my parents didn't have the money to travel and I honestly had no desire up until this trip was made possible. That was when I got excited."

He mumbled something but I couldn't quite hear him.

"What did you say?"

He cleared his throat. "Just to check in before and after you talk to Diane."

"Will do. I plan on scoping out the beach today and start fresh tomorrow."

"Enjoy yourself and if you need anything, call."

"Thanks, boss."

I hung up with Nash and quickly dialed Omar's number before I lost the nerve. I couldn't explain why I felt nervous, but I did. My anxiety became nonexistent when it went straight to voicemail.

"Hey, Na——Omar. Sorry——I just hung up with Nash." I smacked my forehead. *I'm so stupid.* "I just wanted to call and let you know that I made it safe and sound. I'm going to head to the beach for a bit. Talk to you later."

I hit the End button, put my phone in my cover-up's pocket, along with my keycard, and headed to the water. I'd take some pictures and send them to Jack and my parents.

The minute I stepped onto the sand, I took my flip-flops off. I dug my toes into the hot, gritty particles. *Pure bliss.* I looked out over the crashing waves and released all the stress that I had been holding on to. The mixture of green and browns colored the ocean water. It wasn't the tranquil blue of the Caribbean waters. The Atlantic had a more soothing, self-grounding reflection. My worries of Nash and Omar, my job, friends, and family immediately released themselves into the churning sea.

I sat at the water's edge, relishing in the warmth the water brought over my toes. The breeze whipped loose thin wisps of hair from my ponytail. I didn't bother removing them from my face; they would only return. I understood why Floridians dealt with the extreme temperatures. I would too for just one perfect day on the beach. It would make the other three hundred sixty-four days worth it.

There was just something so calming and peaceful about the beach. Even on the most busiest of days, there would only be smiles and laughter from those who chose to spend the day here. I wouldn't actually know that, but what few people I had already encountered were nothing but smiles. There were no words of anger or tension-filled air. It was the most amazing experience that I have ever had. For a brief second, I allowed myself to dream of living right here for the rest of my life.

I brushed the sand off and walked down the beach with no destination in mind. I spotted a tiny food shack a little ways up. My stomach growled at the thought of food. The place looked like a tiki hut, a bamboo gazebo with palm leaves for the roof. I sat down on one of the barstools, dropping my flip-flops onto the sand. Like Kenny Chesney says, *It's a no-shoes nation* or something like that.

The young college age girl threw a bar towel over her shoulder and leaned on her elbows. "What can I get you?"

I took a brief glance at the chalk-written menu that hung over the bar. "I'd love a cheeseburger with lettuce, onion, mayo, and ketchup with a side of fries."

She had no need to write this down; I'm the only customer. So why is she still staring at me?

"Anything to drink?"

Ah, and there it is. I laugh. "I'd love a frozen daiquiri."

"Strawberry or peach mango. Virgin or non?"

So many decisions... What the hell. "Strawberry and with lots of alcohol!"

She nodded and walked around to the back through a swinging door, where I assumed the kitchen was. I twisted in my stool so that my back was to the bar and I faced the water once again. The sound of the blender broke the calming sound of the waves.

"Here you go."

I swiveled back around. "Thanks."

"So what brings you to these parts?"

I took a sip of the cool, refreshing half-frozen liquid. *Sweet, sugar, and with a hint of bite——a perfect drink.* "This is good. A mini-vacation of sorts."

"You came at a good time. The weather is still pretty warm and so is the water. Hurricane season is over, so you won't have to worry about too much rain."

"Wonderful. What would you recommend for some sight-seeing?"

She tapped her slender index finger to her chin. "Amelia Island is just on the other side. It's a short drive with cute stores to shop. Fort Clinch is a couple of miles from here if you want to hike or rent a bike. It also has beach access that isn't crowded because you have to pay to get into the park. It really depends on what you want to do and how long you are staying."

"Not that long––a couple days. Thank you for the information."

She smiled and it made her look even younger. "No problem. And your food will be up in a minute."

I smiled and took another sip of heaven. I reached in my pocket to answer my ringing phone. "'Lo."

"The sunshine and sand must have already worked their magic on you. I can tell that you've adjusted to the beach life."

I smiled and enjoyed the teasing in his tone. "Yep. I'm not wearing any shoes and I don't plan on it for the rest of the day. My plan is to eat this burger that is bigger than my face and finish the most delicious strawberry daiquiri ever."

"Mmm. No shoes, bare legs, and a big fat burger. My mouth is watering."

Mine was too and not because of the food. His words conjured up some wicked images of his talented mouth.

"Keep it PG. I'm out in public."

"Why, Skye, are you blushing?"

I actually giggled. "No. I never blush." *Maybe just a little!*

His howling was infectious and in no time, I was snorting with laughter. "How was work?" I asked, trying to rein in the conversation.

"I have a late shift. I don't go in until eleven tonight."

"Oh my gosh. I am sorry——you should have slept in this morning."

"I went back to bed after you left. I got up a little bit ago."

"Good. For a minute, I felt bad."

"No you didn't."

I could feel his smile through the phone.

"You're right. I didn't feel bad about it at all."

"You go enjoy your meal. How about I call you in the morning after my shift?"

I know he couldn't see my illuminating smile but it warmed me from head to toe. "Sounds good. I've got some scouting to do tomorrow before I ambush the aunt. You can keep me company."

"I like the sound of that. Have a good night."

"You, too. Talk to you tomorrow."

"Bye."

I hung up and stared at my uneaten food. I didn't want to break the spell that he had cast over me. He made me feel giddy, smart, beautiful, and wanted. With him, I didn't have to question where I stood. His body and his words were out there for me to see. He didn't hide his emotions. It was a total one-eighty from Nash. Nash hid every emotion except when he felt caged and then he lashed out, creating destruction in his wake. I hated when I constantly questioned myself in Nash's presence. With Omar, it was easy. There was no pretense, just open and easy companionship. His eyes gave away everything that he was feeling and thinking. He was absolutely refreshing. I seriously considered having him come down and spend the weekend with me.

With a renewed hunger, I demolished every morsel of that burger and fries. My belly was full and my head a little lighter from the alcohol. I was feeling optimistic about this trip and my future conversation with the aunt.

CHAPTER 19

I QUICKLY DRESSED AND HEADED TO my car. I plugged in Diane's address into the car's GPS and headed in the direction that the robotic woman instructed. I wove in and out of small neighborhoods before the GPS told me that I had arrived at my destination. I slowed the car enough to make sure that the address on the mailbox matched what I had inputted into the GPS.

I drove past and parked on the side road. Luckily for me, there was a For Sale sign in the yard of the house I had stopped in front of. An excellent cover for me to remain inconspicuous. This area seemed more like a year-round residency. The places along the beach were more for tourists renting for a week and then moving on. That's what I surmised from the weekly rental yard signs that littered a majority of the houses' lawns.

I pretended to be preoccupied with writing down information while I kept one eye trained on Diane's house. A black Honda remained parked in the drive. I glanced at my watch. It was only eight. The local bank opened up at nine. I still had time before she headed to work. Her house was a pretty good size. The yard was dusted with sand, with thick patches of grass poking through. It wasn't the type of grass you'd want to go barefoot in. It looked as if it would tear at the delicate skin of your soles. It was a beautiful shade of emerald but lacked the soft texture of Kentucky bluegrass from home.

The house was one story and built of cinder. On the outside, the house had no character; it was painted a cold white, void of any rich color hues. There were no bushes or colorful flowers to mark a stunning transition from the yard to the house. Everything on the outside fell flat and dismal. The only distinctive color was from the front door and even that was a deep mahogany brown. It stood out from the rest of the home. The door had opened and a plain woman in black dress paints and a faint blue top emerged. She carried her keys in one hand and her purse hung off her shoulder. Just as with the house, there was nothing that stood out. It was as though she purposely wanted to blend in. Her car flashed its lights and beeped once as she unlocked it and got inside. I watched her back out. She passed me at the regulated speed of the street. I waited a minute before I followed.

She pulled into Trust Bank and parked. I pulled past and headed toward the hotel. Her shift was over at five, so I dialed the Realtor and made an appointment for five thirty. Until then, the shops at Amelia Island called my name. But first a quick call to Nash.

"Morning, boss."

"What's up, Briggs?"

He sounded more cheery today. *Thank God.* I hated talking to his cold persona.

"I just watched Diane head to work. I've got an

appointment later this evening to look at a house that is close to hers."

"You thinking of moving?" He chuckled at his own joke.

"Ha, you wish. Just trying to get a better feel for this woman. See if anyone else lives there."

"Good plan. Are you going to follow her for a couple of days before you go and speak with her?"

I pulled my bottom lip in. "Not sure yet."

"What's your plan for the rest of the day?"

"Tour the island, maybe bring you back a trinket or two." I grinned. I liked this side of our relationship.

"I want a flip-flop keychain."

I busted out laughing and for Pete's sake, that's exactly what he was going to get. I could just imagine that thing dangling from his key set.

"If you're a good boy and stay out of trouble." I had a hard time getting the words out because of my laughter.

His voice dipped an octave. "I've been a very good boy."

Fuck! I shouldn't have even teased him like that. *Damn him and his innuendos that would never come to fruition.* It only pissed me off that I would keep doing this to myself.

"Okay, boss. I've got to hit the shops. Talk to you later."

I hit the End button before he could respond. I slammed the palms of my hands on the steering wheel. *Damn, damn, damn.*

I walked to the front desk, berating myself the entire time. I put a smile on my face and more pep in my step, bound and determined to forget the way that he made me melt from his voice alone. The desk clerk was talkative and gave me detailed directions to Amelia Island.

I parked on the side street and fed the meter. I gave myself two hours to stroll and window-shop. The town wasn't large by any means but it had history and I wanted to soak it all in. The streets were lined with specialty shops. I decided to start at one end and then work my way back. There were flashy boutiques, typical tourist shops, and my favorite, a small bookstore. I hardly ever physically turned pages any more, but I couldn't resist the pull of all the spines calling out to me.

The shopkeeper smiled and welcomed me to her store. I smiled back, knowing that I wouldn't walk out of here without a book in my hands. This wasn't Barnes and Noble but the selection was decent. I picked two out of at least fifty that I could have easily purchased. Of course, one was a romance and the other was a blend of mystery and love. I was a sucker for both. I rarely read tragic stories; I wanted a happily-ever-after ending.

I paid for my purchases and continued on my journey. On my way back around, I spotted a novelty store that would for sure have the keychain for Nash. I stepped in and it was exactly what I had imagined that they would have. They sold beach glassware, wooden painted signs, and keychains and other hodgepodge stuff. I spun the rack until I found a pair of pink painted metal flip-flops. *Sorry, Nash, no other colors!* I picked up my find and spotted a blown-glass aqua and green turtle. Jack would love the intricate details and she would find just the right spot for it. I hoped that she loved it as much as I did. The next rack over were aprons; I spotted the one that said Kiss the Cook. It was cheesy and Omar need it to complete his wardrobe while cooking. I picked it up and stared at it as I contemplated that purchase. I warred internally until I gently hung it back on the rack.

I left the store, elated with the gifts that I had picked out. I crossed the street and headed to the ice cream shop. The smells of homemade fudge, cookies, and lattes forced me to inhale an eager lungful of fragrant air. I hit the lottery on this one. I took my pralines and cream cone and pumpkin latte, and sat on the metal bench. Safely tucked into my purse were a dozen snickerdoodle cookies for later.

I looked at the time. I had three hours left before I had to meet the Realtor. Back to the beach I went. I wanted to get as much of that in before I left. There was no telling when or if I would be back. If I could bottle it all up and take it with me, I would. I remembered the salesperson at the novelty shop had told me that Fernandina Beach was the best place to find sharks teeth. I snagged a tiny bag from the front desk of the hotel and sprinted to the beach. I was on a mission and I wasn't leaving until I found at least one.

I was on my hands and knees, sifting through the sand, when my phone rang. I plopped on to my butt, wiped my wet hands, and answered the call.

"Hello," I huffed out, beyond frustrated.

"You're on the beach. Shouldn't you be happy?" His teasing tone already brightened my spirits.

"That's the problem. I'm combing the beach for shark's teeth. Actually, I've been in one spot for an hour. My knees hurt from the broken shells that I've been kneeling on and I haven't found one flipping tooth."

His laughter at my petty problem didn't make me any angrier. In fact, it had the opposite effect.

"I'm so lame." I pretend pouted.

"You are adorable."

I chuckled sarcastically. "Thanks, I think." The water lapped at my toes and I relaxed into the conversation. "Did you get some sleep?"

"I did. It was a long shift and I'm glad it's over. Have you spoken with the aunt yet?"

"No. I went by her house and followed her to work. I've got an appointment later to walk through a house just down from hers."

"What's your plan?"

"That's the funny part. I really don't have one."

"You just going to wing it?"

I guffawed. "Pretty much."

"Make sure you carry your piece. You may need it."

"Omar, I flew out here. I can't bring a weapon on an airplane." I was shocked that he, of all people, suggested that.

"Go buy a knife or something, just in case."

I grinned at his silliness, but he was right. "Will do. Thanks, Dad."

"Such a smartass."

"You love it."

"I wouldn't have you any other way. Go back to your search and call me later."

"Yes, sir."

"I kind of like that."

"I bet you do. Bye."

"Later."

I gave up looking for those tiny ass teeth. I brushed the sand off and headed to my room to get ready for the walk-through.

CHAPTER 20

I SMILED AND GREETED THE OLDER gentleman with thinning hair. He was paunchy, with a fleshy handshake. He took his handkerchief out of his front pocket and wiped the beaded sweat from his wide forehead. I wondered whether he had another handkerchief for me. It was blazing hot and not a breeze in sight. I glanced over my shoulder and Diane's driveway sat empty.

"Shall we go in?" I prodded.

I moved him on a little so that we could get into cooler air. I was afraid that we would both perish in the sweltering heat. I sighed with relief as soon as we stepped through the door. *Sweet Jesus, the twenty-degree drop in temperature felt wonderful.* I glanced at my watch. Another ten minutes or so and Diane should be pulling into her drive.

I half-heartedly listened to his spiel about the house. I followed him around the home, answered when asked a question, and offered generic comments about the house. The house was cute but needed Jack's touch. Not that I would be purchasing this house. If I could ever afford it, I would buy one right on the beach. It would have its own beachfront access and a wall of glass windows on the side that offered the view of the ocean. He went to the kitchen to sit and told me to take my time. I went directly to the family room and looked out the window. This spot gave me the perfect view of her house.

Diane's car sat in the exact spot in the drive as this morning. *Damn, I had missed her return.* I went to turn back around and an older Chevy compact car pulled in next to hers. I pulled out my cell phone and switched on the camera. A young woman with long brown hair stepped out. I couldn't get a great picture from this angle or tiny lens. *Shit!* I needed my camera that sat in a locked drawer back at the office. I snapped a quick couple of pictures of the woman's back. I'd scrutinize over them later. I turned around and headed back to the Realtor.

"I think I'm done here."

He stood and we shook hands. He gave me his card. "Let me know if you have any more questions or want another walk-through."

I nodded. "Thank you for your time. I'll be in touch."

I wouldn't, but he didn't need to know that. What I wanted to do was peer in Diane's windows or canvass the house from my car and wait for the woman to leave so that I could get a good picture of her. Instead, I headed back to the hotel.

I ordered room service. While I waited, I called Nash.

As soon as he answered, I spit out the new information. "I spotted a young woman, maybe in her early twenties or younger. I couldn't be sure. All I could get was a shot of the back of her. There really is no telling how old she is. Do you think that we can get a picture of what Gray might look like now?"

"It's a possibility. I know a guy who could probably handle that. Did you see anything else?"

"No."

"It might not be her," he said softly.

I deflated. "I know but I want it to be so badly."

"I know you do. Keep canvassing the house before you talk to her. If it is Gray, you don't want the aunt to scare her off. If she is hiding her, it's for a good reason."

"I was afraid you'd say that." I huffed out a frustrated breath. "You don't know how bad I want to go to that house right now and demand entrance."

"I do and that's precisely why you won't," he said with finality.

"I won't." My eyes rolled to the ceiling. This was beyond aggravating. The knock at the door gave me an excuse to get off the phone. "I've got to go, room service is here."

"Talk to you later."

I threw my phone on the bed and answered the door.

"Where would you like this?" the kid, maybe in his early twenties, asked.

"Just put it over by the TV."

I took some cash out of my wallet and handed it to him.

"Thanks."

I moved the tray over to the small desk, grabbed my phone, and sat down to eat. I opened the picture app and enlarged the picture. I analyzed it while I chewed half-heartedly on some French fries.

Damn it! The quality of the picture was terrible. I couldn't discern anything from it. The distance for a decent picture was too far and the screen from the window I was standing behind blurred the rest of the details. All I got was a woman about my height, straight brown hair, and a slender build. Which told me absolutely zilch. This could be Gray or a shitty description of a hundred other women out there. I couldn't catch a break for the life of me. *What was I doing wrong and what have I not thought of? Come on, Skye, think out of the box.*

Nothing; I thought of absolutely nothing. I would do another drive-by in the morning and the evening. That was it and then I would go speak with Diane. Once I made up my mind, I finished my dinner and actually tasted the food. It wasn't as good as the burger I had from the place on the beach but still tasty.

The next two days of scouting was a big fat waste of my time. She had no other visitors. I blew out a puff of air as I walked the beach. A storm was on the horizon. The angry blackness of the clouds was exactly how I was felt. With every crash of the waves, my mind churned. The tiny drops of rain did nothing to cleanse my thoughts. I hadn't talked to Nash. What was the point? I had no new information. Tonight, I was determined to speak with Diane and then hop a plane home. I didn't care whether I stirred up more shit. This was exactly what the case needed. If the woman was Gray, then she might go into hiding again. If I was right, then I just stepped on a hornet's nest.

I picked up my phone and dialed Lisa. "Hey,

Lisa. I need you to book me a flight out tomorrow morning."

"You done with the sun and sand already?" Her intended sarcasm didn't hit its mark.

"Sure am. There is only so much time you can spend eating burgers and drinking daiquiris before it gets old."

"Are you sick?"

My laughter sounded hollow. "No. Pissed is the word for it. I'm ready to come home."

"I'm looking right now and I can get you a flight for ten."

"Go ahead and book it. Thanks, Lisa."

"FYI, I'm glad you're coming home. The boys have been in a mood since you left."

"They just miss me giving them shit. I'll be back in time to give them all hell."

"Good. Looking forward to it. See you tomorrow."

"Bye."

I gave Diane plenty of time to get home and settled before I knocked on her door. There was only one light that shone in the house; the rest was dark and vacant-looking. I pounded on the door again when no one answered. I finally heard footsteps. I took a step back and waited.

The door cracked open. The chain prohibited the door from opening wider.

"Diane?"

"What can I help you with?"

"I'm Skye Briggs with Donovan Investigations and I would like to come in and speak with you about Gray."

The door shut and I held my breath, praying

that she'd open it back up. I released my breath when I heard the scrape of metal against metal as the chain was removed.

"Come on in." Her voice was gruff with annoyance.

I followed quickly before she changed her mind. Her home was nothing like the outside. It was cozy and inviting. She had decorated the living room with rich brown hues. We stepped through the cheery and bright kitchen.

She pulled out a chair, never offering me a drink. I never expected her to, as this was the opposite of a friendly visit.

She put her elbows on the table. "I'm surprised it took you this long to talk to me."

"The detective never spoke with you?"

"No. No one did."

I knew that but it still shocked me to hear it. The ineptitude of the police force, excluding Omar, was astounding. Yet, they inadvertently provided me with a job security.

"What can you tell me about Gray's disappearance?"

She stared at her folded hands. "Unfortunately, not much."

"Anything you can think of will help, I assure you." I tried to give her a reassuring smile but it fell flat.

"All I know is that Gray went home sick and when Penny came back from work, she was gone."

Her shoulders sagged with guilt, defeat, or maybe a touch of both.

"How well do you know Harold?"

Her shoulders straightened and a scowl glared

back at me. *Wow.* That was a quick change of demeanor. She didn't have to say anything. I could feel the waves of her abhorrence settle between us.

"He is a son-of-a-bitch. He treats my sister like she is beneath him. He controls every aspect of her life. I wouldn't be surprised if he was the one who killed Gray."

"Do you believe that Gray is dead?"

She looked through me with agonized conviction. "Without a doubt."

"How can you be so sure?"

"If you knew Harold like I do, then you would believe that too."

"What about Penny? Does she believe that her daughter is dead and that Harold may have had something to do with it?"

Her heavy sigh made her body shrink into itself. "She is in denial. She is afraid of him and won't do anything to make her situation worse."

"What do you mean by that––make her situation worse?"

"He physically beats her and lowers her self-worth to the point that she won't stand up to him or leave him. She is afraid of what he would do to her if she did."

"Do you think that he would harm her if she left him? Have you tried to intervene? Coax her and Gray to come and live with you?" I fired the questions at her.

"I've tried everything. The last time I was there, I begged and pleaded with her to leave him. To run but she wouldn't. I even tried using Gray as incentive to leave with me. I offered to take Gray with me until she could get away. She refused, said that he would find them and that they would always be looking over their shoulder."

"Have you ever witnessed Harold abusing Penny?"

"Not physically, but I have seen some bruises and heard the names that he has called her."

"Have you kept in contact with your sister since you last saw her?"

"The last time I talked to her was when she told me that Gray went missing. I washed my hands of her. She wouldn't take my help when I offered. What more could I have done?" She stared off in space with dry eyes.

"Was Harold always abusive toward Penny?"

"That's the sad part. It wasn't until after Gray was born that I noticed it. When they had first married, they seemed like the perfect match. They seemed so in love. I actually liked him in the beginning and thought that he was a good man."

"What do you think changed?"

She shook her head. "I'm not sure. The only thing that I can think of that was different was Gray."

Did she know about the affair and was purposely lying about it? Did Penny keep that from her sister?

"Did Penny ever work outside the home before she began volunteering?"

"She did, but I can't remember where. As far as I understood, she quit to stay home with Gray."

"Are you close with your sister?"

"We were at one time. I couldn't wait to be an

aunt and spoil her child rotten. I didn't plan on having any family of my own. I was elated with Gray's arrival."

"So you distanced yourself because of Harold? Don't you think that she needed you even more?"

That was a shitty thing to say but it was true. *How could she walk away and not continue to fight until Penny and Gray were away from Harold?*

A couple of tears ran down her cheeks. "There aren't many things that I regret but leaving Penny and Gray was one of my biggest mistakes. If I had tried harder maybe Gray would still be with us. If I pushed more, I might still have them both in my life."

I placed my hand over hers. I could feel the slight tremble. "I'm sorry. I know this is hard on you. I hate to ask these questions and dredge up the past, but I want to find out what happened to Gray."

She looked into my eyes pleadingly. "Harold has all the answers."

I nodded, taking her seriously. Harold was a bastard and I couldn't discount the fact that he had something to do with his child's disappearance. I was even more frustrated than before. I had hoped that Penny had hidden Gray with Diane, but she seemed convinced that Harold had killed Gray.

I stood and handed her my card. "Thank you for taking the time to speak with me. Please call me if you think of anything else." I paused and turned back around. "I will find her one way or another."

"I hope you do," she said, barely above a whisper.

She didn't get up to walk me out and I didn't expect her to. I had dredged up enough shit. I left her sitting at the kitchen table, looking lost in a sea of memories.

CHAPTER 21

I WALKED INTO THE OFFICE AND a smiling Lisa greeted me. Her presence alone brightened up the place. It was nice to have another female around the office. Nash was right: she was organized, efficient, and tough. She fit in well with the rest of the team. Plus, every Monday she brought in homemade peanut butter cookies that melted in your mouth.

"Are there any cookies left or did the guys scarf them down?"

"It's Friday." She laughed.

I chuckled. "You're right. The guys gobble them down before you even have a chance to put them out on a plate. A girl can hope, though!"

She winked. "I put some in the freezer just for you. Take them home tonight."

I rushed over and hugged her. "I love you."

She giggled and patted my back like a child.

"I'm trying a new recipe. I'll bring them in Monday."

I grinned. "I'll be your guinea pig anytime. I've got to check in with the boss."

She shooed me away and I chuckled the whole way to Nash's office.

He looked up briefly from his desk then back

down to whatever he was reading.

"Well hello to you, too." Sarcasm dripped from every word.

His lips barely twitched. He wanted to smile but wouldn't dare let me see it. "You're back earlier than I expected. Did you talk to Diane?"

"I did. She pointed her finger at Harold. She swore that he killed her."

"What do you think?"

"I think that there is legitimacy to that but seeing the young woman also makes me believe that she is lying."

He held out a piece of paper. I snatched it from his grip, greedy to look at its contents. "Is this what Gray might look like now?"

"That's what the computer generated."

"I can't compare the two. Her hair color is lighter now. She very well could've dyed it or they are sun streaks." I blew out a puff of air. "I didn't see her face. I want to believe that there is a likeness but that might be wishful thinking on my part."

He passed me another file.

"What's this?"

"More cases that have come in. I handled your other clients. You've become quite popular with the cheating partner crowd."

"Yes, just what I was aiming for! You didn't have to do that."

"I also put the check for them in your desk drawer."

My eyes went as round as my mother's china plates. "What! I won't take it. I didn't earn it. I'll rip them up once I get in there," I shouted at him.

He banged his fists on the desk and I jumped at the sudden harshness.

"They were easy cases and I had the time. I am the fucking boss and I will do what I damn well please." He softened his voice. "Skye, please take the money. The cases were technically yours." He held up his hand. "Before you say anything, I would have done the same thing for the guys. We all work as a team here."

"Yeah, but I don't give Ryker or Hawke money if I take one of their cases."

"Let it go," he demanded.

So, I did. I wasn't happy about it, but there was no use in trying to argue with him. As he stated, *he was the boss.*

"Fine, but I don't like it," I huffed.

"You don't have to." His voice was almost a whisper. "By the way, I like the sun-kissed look."

I lowered my head before he could see my cheeks redden. *Damn him!* "Thanks."

Why did I come back? Oh yeah, I had bills to pay and a girl to find. I went back to my office and scanned the file that Nash had given me. More cheating cases. I swear, that this office made most of its money from deceitful scum. For once, I wanted to see a happy ending. *Was that too much to ask for?*

I sent a quick text to Omar.

I'm home—want to grab a bite to eat?

I set the phone down and made a couple of quick calls to start the ball rolling on the new cases. Until I figured out my next move, I would fill my time with petty cheaters. I left later than I had expected and had yet to hear back from Omar. So, I hit the drive-thru at the first fast-food joint that I came to. A ninety-nine cent heart attack was just what the doctor ordered. I didn't want to fill up too much just in case Omar decided to text me back. I hadn't talked with him in a couple of days and didn't know his work schedule. He could still be working the night shift. By ten, I gave up and ate some of Lisa's cookies and then went to bed.

I woke to the ringing of my phone. "Hello?" I drowsily answered.

There was no answer. I asked again, this time angrier. "Hello?"

All I could hear on the other end was a swishing sound. I looked at the time: six in the morning. *Give me a flipping break.* I hung up the phone, disgusted with the caller's butt dial. I didn't recognize the number so I flopped back on the mattress and fell back asleep. After what felt like only a minute of extra sleep, the phone rang again.

"What?" I shouted into the mouthpiece.

"Good morning, sunshine!"

"Morning. Sorry about that. I had a butt dial before you, and I was trying to fall back asleep."

"Do you need to go back to the sunshine state? You seem to have left it all there."

"Har-de-har-har. Are you always this hilarious in the morning?"

"Well, I was going to ask you to breakfast, but on second thought, I'll wait until lunch. Why don't you call me back later?"

"I'm sorry. How about we meat up at the Mexican place on the corner of Hunter and Main Street around noon."

"See you there."

"Later."

I hated being a bitch to Omar when he was so nice. If we took this relationship further, he needed to be aware of my morning mood swings. Anything less than six full hours and I was snarky. Mornings and I had a love-hate relationship. I did apologize, so I felt better as I curled back up in my comforter.

I groggily reached for the phone again in what seemed like five minutes later. I looked at the caller ID and of course it was an unknown number.

Oh for fuck's sake! "This is Skye."

"You better quit digging up old information." The voice sounded computerized.

I was wide awake now. "What information are you talking about?"

"You know exactly what I'm talking about. Keep looking for answers and you'll be the next to die."

I straight up laughed at the caller. I didn't give a flying rat's ass. No one was going to threaten me or scare me off the case.

"Yeah, okay. I'll quit digging."

The line had clicked dead so my famous line fell on deaf ears. Whoever was trying to scare me off did not do their job. I was more determined than ever. I was pushing buttons and it wouldn't be long before someone screwed up and I had all the answers.

I dialed Nash. "Hey, boss. I just received a threatening call on my life if I don't quit looking for answers."

That got his attention.

"What did they say and what did they sound

like? What was the number?"

"I just told you the gist of what they said. I couldn't tell if the caller was male or female. It was one of those voice-box sounding machines. The number was blocked."

"Keep your firearm on you at all times. Let me know when you leave the house and where you are going."

"You going to put a tail on me? Put a tracker in my purse? Come on, Nash. We both know that if he or she were planning on hurting me, none of those things will keep me safe. I'll carry everywhere I go. I'll even put it in my waistband holster and not in my purse if that will make you feel better."

I grinned at the ease of pissing him off.

"Skye, this is fucking serious. That person could be anyone."

"I know it's serious. How dumb do you think that I am? I will protect myself. I got another session with Ryker tomorrow and I'll be with Omar this afternoon. He is a cop and well-armed."

"Who's the cop? Were you dating before or after I kissed you?" he all but shouted into the phone.

My hackles rose, but I managed to stay calm. "Not that it's any of your business, but his name is Omar Montejo. And for your last stupid question, no, we were not dating at the time."

"How the hell do you expect him to protect you?"

"Look, Nash, you have told me many times that whatever chemistry we have will not be acted upon. What would you have me do? Pine away for something that will never come to fruition?

Please! Let's move past this right now. I'm already tired of it."

"Fine. Tell your boyfriend about your caller so that he is aware of the situation."

He ended the call.

I flipped my phone over and looked at the home screen. *Did that really happen?* He had no right to be jealous. He had a multitude of opportunities to take it further and he was all but stomped on the brakes. I'd be damned if I wasted any more time obsessing over him.

I stomped through the house as our conversation played on a continuous loop through my head. I had to get my head straight before I met up with Omar. I wouldn't let Nash fuck with a good thing. I let all thoughts of Nash wash down the drain as I showered. Okay, I was still pissed but felt better than I did earlier.

Omar drew me in for a scorching kiss.

"Yum. I'm having second thoughts about lunch." I grinned mischievously.

"Real food first and then dessert."

"Spoilsport."

We sat in the red vinyl booth in the back. I was learning that every time we went out, he made sure to face the door. It was something that I would have to learn. I normally didn't pay attention to my surroundings but if I were to keep safe, I needed to start doing a better job.

I picked up a chip and smothered it with the spicy salsa. It had just the right hint of heat.

"How was your trip?"

I covered my mouth as I chewed. "It was productive. The aunt pointed the finger at the father. She was adamant that Gray was dead. I also spotted a young woman going into her home one evening. She never came back but I think it might be Gray. Oh, and I got a call this morning saying that if I didn't quit searching, then I was going to die."

He choked on his chip.

"Are you all right?" I asked concerned.

"Yeah. What do you mean you had a threatening call this morning?" He coughed again.

"Exactly what I said. Why is that so hard to believe?"

"It's not that I don't believe you. It's concerning that you get a call after you go to Florida, dredging up the past. Someone found out and is pissed. Do you think the father knows that you went?"

"I don't think so. Diane and Penny aren't speaking and she hates Harold. How would he find out?"

"That's the million-dollar question."

"Diane could've called Penny after I had spoken with her. Knowing how controlling Harold is, he very well could have forced Penny to tell him."

"Why don't you stay with me for a couple of days?"

"Thank you for the offer but I don't need you to babysit me."

His head whipped up and his dark eyes looked black. "You really think that?"

Crap, I'd just pissed him off. "I didn't mean it like that and you know it. I can take care of myself."

He placed his hand over mine. His eyes softened. "I know you can. I simply wanted you to know that I am here for you and if you feel more comfortable with me around, then I would love to have you stay." He picked up my hand and kissed the back of it. "I would make it worth your time."

I laughed out loud. "I might take you up on a night here and there. If you play your cards right."

Lust danced in his delicious brown eyes. "I may have an ace or two up my sleeve."

He let go of my hand as the waiter brought our lunch.

Before for he took his first bite, he said, "Seriously though, keep me in the loop if you get any more threatening calls."

"I will." I smiled and stabbed my fork into a piece of chicken.

I moaned in pleasure as the spices teased my taste buds. "This is so good," I said around a mouthful of shredded chicken and peppers.

"You should taste my mom's tamales. Those are scary good."

I nodded and kept shoveling in more food so I didn't have to comment. Meeting his parents was nerve-racking at the moment and I wanted to enjoy his company before I had to think about meeting his family.

CHAPTER 22

MY BACK SLAMMED AGAINST THE wall as he pushed me up against it. He ravaged my mouth, only pulling away to remove my shirt. His skilled hands unclasped my bra quicker than I ever could. His soft lips seared a path along my jaw and down my neck. My fingers pulled at his thick strands as he drove my body crazy.

This man was going to be the death of me. He was sweet, sincere, and a skilled lover. Sure, he was younger than me but with that came stamina! He knew how to treat a woman in the bedroom or, in my case, up against the wall. I shut my brain down and let my body feel all of the glorious things that his hand and mouth were creating.

He had stripped me down with finesse.

"Spread 'em, Skye. Show me your beautiful pussy," he commanded.

Oh my word! His husky voice and hot breath hovering over my vagina made my knees weak, but I obeyed his command.

His tongue lashed out and licked my most sensitive area. I bucked at the sensation of his wet tongue circling my clit. My body rode the pulsating waves until I cried out his name. My legs shook from the violent storm that had crashed through me. He held me against the wall, kissing his way up to my breasts. I panted as the need to have him inside of me threatened to shatter my existence.

He teased and tormented each bud until they were razor-sharp. I moved my head from side to side, not sure that I could take any more of his sensual assault.

"Omar." I gasped as he flicked the overly sensitive peak.

"Yes, *mi reina*," he answered with an aching voice from holding back his own need.

I had no idea what the fuck he was calling me but it sounded sexy and it drove me even crazier.

"Fuck me," was all that I was able to voice.

He slipped out of his jeans and kicked them to the side. His thick cock twitched as he gazed at me. "You are so beautiful. Are you ready to be fucked?"

I nodded. "Please," I begged.

"Wrap your legs around me."

I did as I was told. The minute my legs wrapped around his waist, the head of his shaft demanded entrance. I draped my arms around his neck and held on as he thrust into me fully. He brought his lips to my neck, softly nibbling as his thrusts increased. My moaning increased as his thumb encircled my clit. I don't know how he managed to hold me up with one arm but I didn't care. I was already teetering off the ledge.

"Open your eyes. I want you to see me when you come." His voice was strained.

I lifted my lids and peered into a tiny bit of his soul. He was so open and giving me a glimpse of what he was thinking. I soaked in the sensual tenderness that gazed back at me. I kissed him with the same fierceness of the orgasm that sliced through my core, his own release in tandem with mine. He left my body as gracefully as he had entered it, as though I were a temple to be worshiped.

We lazily gathered our clothes and dressed.

He turned on the TV and asked whether I wanted a glass of wine. "Yes, please."

He handed me a chilled glass of red and sat next to me.

"What does *mi reina* mean?" I peered into my glass of wine, praying that they were words of a pet name and not something derogative.

His mouth curved with tenderness. "It means my queen."

I felt a warm glow flow through me and it wasn't from the wine. He opened his arm invitingly and I snuggled into his side. We both were lost in our own thoughts. In the span of a couple of hours our relationship had gone from casual to devastatingly intimate.

"How is the case coming along?"

I shrugged off my anxious thoughts, feeling more comfortable with talk around things that I could control.

"It's slow and frustrating. I'm desperate to find out what happened. If that phone call this morning told me anything, it was that I am getting closer to those answers."

"Is risking your life in the process worth it?" His voice took on a serious tone.

Tilting my head back, I peered coolly at his face.

He quirked his eyebrow questioningly. "Does it?"

"What if it were your daughter, or sister, or mother who had gone missing? Wouldn't you do everything that you could to find them, regardless if it cost you your life? Don't you put your life in danger every time you step into your uniform?" I rapidly fired back.

I noted his set face, his clamped mouth and fixed eyes. I gently placed my hand along his clenched jaw and softened my voice. "There is no difference between me doing my job and you doing yours."

He pressed a kiss in my palm before he replyed. "Doesn't mean that I like you in harm's way."

"I know. I don't have a death wish, just a small obsession with finding this girl."

I relaxed measurably as a grin overtook his features. "If you run into trouble, make sure you call me. I've got a whole squad of blue to back you."

"I'm counting on it."

I kissed him thoroughly the next morning, hoping for his neighbors to shout *Get a room!* A shame no one did because as far as good-bye kisses went, that was a make-your-panties-wet kind.

"See you later."

"I'll call you after my shift this afternoon."

I grinned like a schoolgirl with her first crush. I turned and waved as I got in my car. He was good for me; the time that I spent in his company got better and better. I grabbed a quick coffee on the way home. I planned on doing nothing until I had to meet up with Ryker tonight. I dreaded his torture but each lesson taught me more ways to handle myself. I would never be a deadly machine with my bare hands like they were. However, I could inflict major damage.

I had just finished mopping the sweat off my face when Ryker walked back through the gym doors.

I put the towel down and looked up at him. "What did you forget? I can't handle any more of you tossing me around like a bean bag."

By the way his brows drew together and the pained pinch of his mouth, I knew that something other than my smart mouth was troubling him.

"Seriously, Ryker. What's going on? You are making me nervous."

"I've called a tow truck and they are on their way."

"Okay." I drew the word out, not understanding why he looked as though he was about to murder someone.

"Someone slashed your tires."

I jumped up and ran out of the building to see for myself. I walked around the entire car, checking to make sure that he wasn't playing some cruel joke on me. Every single tire had a huge gash in the sidewall. Along both sides of the vehicle, written in blood-red, was *Die Bitch*. I could feel Ryker's massive presence behind me. I took comfort in having him close, even as his anger fused to mine.

"Who the fuck would do this?" I looked over my shoulder. "Don't we have cameras outside the building?"

I wasn't afraid. I was fucking pissed. My mom-mobile would take forever in the shop and cost me a ton of money, which I didn't have. How dare that cocksucker ruin my things and then have the balls to flee from the scene. *What, he couldn't face me like a man?*

"I've already checked. Whoever did this smashed the camera with a rock or something. I'm betting that they stayed hidden or covered themselves well so that we couldn't ID them. I'll have Nash pull the tapes. Do you want to be here when he does?"

I threw my hands up in the air and let them crash down to my sides. "No. Can you give me a lift home?"

"Sure. Let me text Nash first and then we can go."

I didn't look at Ryker, just said my thanks, and slammed the car door behind me. I shouldn't have taken my anger out on him or his car. It wasn't his fault that this had happened. I wanted to confront Harold this minute but I had no mode of transportation or proof that it was him. *Shit!* Now I was really pissed off. I'd have to go rent a car and shell out more fucking money. I had it, but that wasn't the point. I hated to see my bank account dwindle on stupid shit.

My phone rang. I looked at the screen to see who was calling and the number was blocked. *Well, looky what we got here. The gall of the son-of-a-bitch.*

"You calling to gloat on your kindergarten

artwork? My dog could do better shit than that."
I snidely spewed the lie.

"I see you got my message. I hope you take it to heart. You will die if you keep digging."

The mechanical voice just sounded so Hollywood thriller and it made a bubble of hysterical laughter escape.

"Is that all you got? 'Cuz, from where I'm standing, you are a cowardly piece of shit that doesn't even deserve my time."

With that said, I hung up the phone. *Fuck him or her.* I wasn't playing their game or by their rules. I wouldn't stand down or give up. I was going to finish what I started. The phone rang again with the same blocked caller. *Nope, not going to even do it.* I left it on the coffee table and let it ring and ring. With shaking hands, I poured a glass of wine, trying to contain my anger before I went and did something stupid.

I heard a soft knock at the door. I ignored it until it became a loud pounding. I set my glass down harder than I needed. Some of the red liquid sloshed over the rim and onto the counter. I sighed loudly and walked to the front. I flung the wood door open and on the opposite side stood Nash: strong and forbidden. He stepped through the door using his large frame, causing me to step back. He kicked the door shut with his foot. The door slammed and I jumped. *God, I was on edge.* I stood a few paces from him. He crossed his thickly corded arms across the muscular expanse of his chest. His feet were shoulder width apart. He looked as though he was ready to do battle and I didn't know whether it was one I wanted to fight.

"I watched the tapes and I can't tell who it is. They wore a dark hood and I couldn't discern any real features." His hands went to his sides, clenching and unclenching.

"Ryker figured as much. I'm fine, Nash. You didn't have to come here." I managed to keep the tremors from my voice.

He moved with confident strides, only stopping when he was mere inches from me. "Come here." His voice was as warm and gentle as a southern breeze coming off the coast.

I shook my head, but went willingly into his arms. He enveloped me with his strong, firm, and protective limbs. "I got another call just before you knocked on the door," I said meekly into his chest.

He didn't say a word just tightened his hold. I went slack in his arms as all of my defenses pooled at my feet. I didn't have the strength to stand. As my anger ebbed, my body trembled violently. Sheer black fright swept through me. I began to shake again as the fearful images of my death built in my mind. Panic rioted through me as fear gnawed away at my confidence.

"Shh. It's going to be all right. I'll stay as long as you need me." His voice was as soothing as a baby's lullaby.

I nodded my head but what I should have been doing was telling him that I didn't need him and that I didn't want him here. He screwed with my head and heart more than the person who wanted me dead. I had to protect my heart and yet I couldn't force myself to step back from him.

He placed one arm on the back of my thighs and kept the other at the base of my neck as he swept me up in his arms as though I were merely an accessory. He carried me to my bedroom and lay me upon the bed. He removed my shoes and slid in behind me. He brought his arm around my waist and tucked me against his chest. He held onto me as though at any moment I was going to disappear. I didn't have the energy to fight him right now. So, I didn't. Instead, I burrowed deeper into him, letting his earthy scent surround me.

I closed my eyes, knowing that Nash would do everything in his power to keep me safe.

"Thank you," I slurred before I drifted to sleep.

I woke up in the same clothes I had on when Nash had tucked me in. The smell of coffee had my body moving of its own volition. I covered my yawn as I stepped through the small kitchen. I walked behind Nash and rummaged in my cupboard for a mug. I stood to the left of him as I poured the hot and soothing liquid into my cup.

I chanced a look at him and his normal hardness had been replaced with a softer and gentler side. There was no sympathy in his eyes, only understanding. His look rocked me to my foundation.

"Thank you again for being here."

I was being sincere. It was hard telling what would have happened if I had been by myself when the anger subsided and the fear took over.

I plopped down in the seat and leaned over my

steaming mug.

Nash kept his body leaning up against the counter but turned to face me.

"I think that you should stay with Omar for the time being." He spoke through clenched teeth.

He never once looked at me, only stared at his own coffee.

My head rose sharply. "No."

He looked up at me with a tiredness coating his eyes that I had never witnessed before. I felt drawn to him and sorry that I had put him in this situation.

"I think it's for the best. We don't know who is after you. I know you. You will not take a step back from this case and let me or one of the other guys handle it."

"You're damn right I'm not." My voice rose, along with my anger. "Quit treating me like a naïve woman. I understand that the stakes are high but I'm not going to quit."

"The stakes are high. Fuck!" He ran his hand down his face in frustration. "Damn it, Skye. Your life is at stake. Don't you get that?" He hung his head in defeat. "I don't want to lose you."

I stood, more confident than ever, and walked over until I stood in his space. I lifted my hands to touch him but abruptly dropped them. "I'm too stubborn to let anything happen to me. I will take precautions but I will not––and I mean it, Nash––I will not hide." I sighed awkwardly. "Omar knows what's going on. When I do stay the night, he is aware and will keep me protected. That's it, Nash. When I'm home, I have my gun and it will go with me when I'm out. I don't need the three of you ghosting behind me."

He set his coffee cup down. "Go get dressed. We will get you a rental on the company until yours is done."

"Well, it did happen on company property, so I guess you have to pay for the damage too." I winked and sauntered out of the kitchen. I could hear him mumble, but I didn't bother to stop to ask him what it was he said. I chuckled to myself, feeling a ton better.

Before Nash had taken off from the rental place, I pulled the trinket from my pocket. I handed it to him. He stared at the girly keychain lying on the palm of his hand. It was slow to form, but the most glorious smile spread and lit up his entire face. For a brief moment, all of his stress went away and the man before me morphed into one whose life hadn't been tainted by the demons of his past. I grinned, filing away that memory as I stepped around him and got into my rental.

CHAPTER 23

I WENT TO HAROLD'S OFFICE DIRECTLY after I picked up my rental. His secretary informed me that he wasn't in. I told her that I had to discuss some of the elements of a job that I had commissioned him to do. That it was imperative that I spoke with him prior to him beginning the job. She happily gave me directions to a home on the other side of town.

I slammed the car door and marched to where Harold stood, inspecting his work.

"Damn good job for someone who has the morals of a rat," I seethed.

"Thank you on both accounts." His sinister grin did not go unnoticed.

I tried to stop the convulsion of my body but I didn't catch it in time. He spotted the tremor and gobbled it up. *Good to know that my fear excited him.*

"You owe me for the damages to my car," I spat.

"I don't know what you are talking about," he replied, feigning ignorance.

"Sure you do. The slashed tires and the new paint job you decided to do."

He crossed his arms over his chest, widened his stance and laughed. "Do you think that I am that juvenile? If I wanted to hurt you, then I would.

I wouldn't go through all the trouble to hide it." He stepped closer and let his arms hang tensely at his sides. "I would simply put my hands around your throat and strangle the life right out of you in broad daylight."

I desperately wanted to back away from him and his stale coffee breath. It made me nauseous. But I straightened my spine, stood my ground, and controlled my gag reflex.

"What, like you did to your daughter?"

He leaned in closer and gritted his teeth. "I don't have a daughter. And for the last fucking time, I did nothing to Gray. I do not know what happened to her."

He enunciated the last part as though I had trouble understanding English.

"I'll prove that you did. The death threats don't scare me. I will find out the truth."

I stomped back to my car, furious.

"Go ahead and try," he shouted to my retreating back.

"I lied. Your landscaping looks like shit. A monkey with no legs, throwing his own shit, could do a better job," I tossed over my shoulder.

Actually, he did a fabulous job on this yard. It looked downright serene. I loved the fact that he was now second-guessing his work as we speak. *Served that narcissistic bastard right!* I chuckled the whole way back to my office.

I slumped in the chair across from Nash's desk. He looked at me from half-raised lids, waiting for me to speak.

"I confronted Harold a few minutes ago."

He slammed his hands on the desk and stood.

"That was the stupidest move that I've ever heard. What the fuck made you think that was a good idea? Are you trying to end your life? Does it not mean anything to you? Do you think that this is some big fucking joke?" He stomped toward the door and kicked it shut.

I cringed as he towered before me. "No, I don't think that this is a joke. I was pissed, okay! I wanted him to admit to my face that he was behind the vandalism."

He put his hands on his hips. "And did he?"

"He said that if he were going to kill me, he would do it in broad daylight and with his bare hands."

"What part of that makes you think that Harold is not serious?"

"I didn't say that he wasn't serious but it did cause me to conclude that he might not be behind the destruction of my car or the phone calls." I mocked his stance.

He huffed out a frustrated minty breath that fanned my face as he placed his large hands on the armrests of my chair, busting my personal bubble. His glare tore through my bravado and straight to my insecurity. He managed to break down my entire foundation with the intensity of his gaze. I squirmed, both in irritation at how quickly he could dissect me and how hot he was making my body. Any minute, my bones would turn to liquid and I would be begging him to fuck me right in his office.

He stood to his full intimidating height and went and sat behind his desk. "You are a giant pain in my ass."

The smile that he had gifted me took the sting out of his words. I maybe a pain in the ass but he wasn't done putting up with it—yet.

I grinned right back at him. "I'll try to be better. But you and I both know that isn't going to happen."

His guttural laugh barreled out of his sensual mouth. I soaked up every sound and vibration and committed it to memory. Nash hardly cracked a smile, let alone laughed.

"Get out of here, Skye. I've got work to do."

"I'll check in later. I'm going to ruffle some more feathers."

His smile broadened, lighting up his face. Nash was a heart-stopper and I needed to get the hell away from him before I did something unforgiveable. I backed out of his office and practically ran toward mine. I shut the door, logged on to the computer, and pulled up the Internet.

I searched the high schools in the Fernandina area online. Unlike Indiana, there was only one high school in the area where Diane lived. *Score one point for easy rummaging for me.* I pulled up the number and called.

"Fernandina High School, how may I help you?"

"Hello, my name is Skye Briggs and I work for Donovan Investigations. I was wondering if you could send me a list of transfer students or newly enrolled students from two years ago?"

"Can you hold, please?"

"Yes, ma'am."

As the elevator music played in the background, I wondered whether they could give me that information without a warrant. I'm sure it would be public information.

"I'm sorry but I just spoke with the principal and we are not allowed to disclose that information."

"Yes, I understand. Is there anyway that you could possibly mail me a copy of the yearbooks for the past two years?"

I was hanging on a limb, asking that.

"May I ask what this is pertaining to?"

"I am working a missing person's case—a young girl. If you want, you can search Donovan Investigations online and the site will tell you that we are a legitimate private investigation company that works closely with the local police department."

She put me on hold again. I waited a couple of minutes before my hope that I would get the information dwindled. Ten more minutes went by and I really started to panic.

"Ma'am?"

"Yes, I'm still here." I breathed out, not realizing that I had been holding my breath.

"Do I put attention to you or just Donovan Investigations?"

"Bless your heart, thank you so much. Please address it to me so that I get the package directly."

"No problem. I will overnight them. I hope that you find the young girl."

"Me too."

Phew! I don't know how it happened but I hoped I caught a lucky break. If Gray had her name changed, I wouldn't know what it was so the roster wouldn't be that much help. I prayed that she took a yearly picture like the rest of the kids. That was the only way that I could match her to the computer-generated one that I had in my desk drawer.

I ran to Nash's office as another idea hit.

"Nash," I rushed out. "Can you pull credit card statements from two years back for both Penny and Diane?"

"I can't promise you anything but I will see what I can pull."

I ran over to his desk and kissed his cheek. Surprise registered all over his beautiful face. I didn't care. I was on a roll and getting closer; I could feel it.

"I hear that the country club is hosting another big card game tonight. I'm heading over to talk to Penny again."

"Watch your back. I don't have anything going on and I feel like playing cards tonight. I'll keep Harold busy so you can talk to Penny."

"I'd kiss you again but I'd hate for you to get used to that. Thanks."

"Keep your phone on in case you need to book it out of there." He turned serious.

"I will."

I waited until Nash had sent me a text stating that Harold had arrived at the club before I drove out to their house. I watched more paint chips scatter to the ground as I knocked on Penny's door. I guessed that Harold was only good at landscaping designs and not very handy at fixing up his house. You'd think that he would want to keep up appearances. *Or he was too busy beating the shit out of Penny to worry about the state of his home.*

The door opened and the woman staring back at me was a shell of the woman I had seen merely days ago.

"Penny, may I come in and talk with you please?"

She opened the door wider and left me to follow her in. I didn't second-guess her intentions. I quickly followed before I lost the opportunity. She didn't quit walking until she came to another door at the opposite end of the kitchen. She opened it and left me again to follow. I shut the door behind me and stood on the back porch. She sat in a rocker overlooking her lush green backyard. There were no lawn ornaments, just acres of green. The simplicity was breathtaking.

"What do you want, Skye? Don't you think that you have done enough?"

I cocked my head to the side and leaned up against one of the porch pillars diagonal from where she sat. "From where I'm standing, I don't think that I have done enough. I still don't have the answers and I haven't found your daughter."

A slow grin flattened out the tiny wrinkles along her lips.

A creepy feeling swept down my spine. *What kind of game was she playing?*

"I know that Gray is not Harold's child. Is the affair that you had what started this whole thing? Is that when Harold started keeping you as a prisoner and using you as a punching bag?" I wasn't going to sugarcoat anything.

"Ah, the affair." She sighed with defeat. Her

eyes turned cold as she glared at me. "What do you know about love, Miss Briggs? Do you have a man in your life who would lay his own life down to protect yours? How about one who delivers a blow to your face and takes delight in the fact that he broke your nose? Do you have the responsibility to care for a child who is innocent and doesn't deserve the situation that you put them in because of your own sickening fear?"

I wasn't sure she had truly wanted me to answer, so I kept my mouth shut. This wasn't about me; it was about Gray.

"I cheated on my husband. I made a mistake, one that I am still paying for. I thought that when Gray was born, Harold would overlook my shortcomings and love her as his own. In reality, he became a cold and bitter man. He hated my beautiful little girl with every ounce of his being. No matter what I did, his hate grew stronger. Yes, he physically and emotionally abuses me but I took all of that for Gray. So she wouldn't endure his wrath. She never did. Despite what we went through at home, Gray was and is loved. I did everything in my power to protect her."

"You didn't do enough because if you did, I wouldn't be standing right where I am. You would still have your daughter. Where is she, Penny?"

She hung her head as tears wracked her body. I don't know whether she cried for her shitty life or the loss of her daughter.

"I don't know. If I did, I would be with her right now." She sniffed into her chest.

"I'm calling your tears and your words bullshit. You are the biggest coward of them all. I will find out what the hell happened to her. I will not stop."

I couldn't stand to be here any longer as lies spewed out of her mouth. I stomped around the house and got in my car. The audacity of her to think that I would believe her sob story. In the beginning, without a doubt, I would have. Now, I knew better. Before I drove off, I sent Nash a text.

I'm out, thanks.

I'm going to stick around and see if I can learn anything.

Let me know if you do.

I tossed my phone on the passenger seat and gunned the engine. I wanted to be as far from this place as I could.

I pulled in Omar's drive and sat with the engine idling. *He wasn't expecting me. Was it right for me to be here? Screw it.* I shut off the car and banged on his door.

He opened the door, shocked to see me on the other side.

I didn't even think about my next move. My body had a mind of its own and it desperately needed Omar. I stood on the tips of my toes and fused my hungry mouth to his. He readily answered with a passion of his own. I wrapped my legs tightly around his waist as he picked me up and kicked the door shut. Our mouths continued to devour each other. I had never felt such a carnal need for someone. It was a terrifying and yet an exhilarating feeling. He walked us over to the couch, where he tossed me on to the cushions. It was exactly what I wanted. I needed him to take charge, to take my thinking away, and to just feel.

He stripped me out of my clothing and quickly

discarded his own. He lay over my heated body and pushed inside until I cried out from the onslaught of pleasure. There was no foreplay or love, just animalistic and primal fucking. He ground his hips with every thrust and moaned as he pushed my body to a height that just might break me. I matched his pace and then forced him deeper and harder. I relished in the tiny slivers of pain. The small twinges soon gave way and my pleasure soared. I screamed his name as my pussy clenched and my orgasm liquefied my body.

I could feel him soften as he pulled away. I felt thoroughly used and spent. He pulled me tightly to his chest, while his fingers created a delicious dance through the strands of my hair.

"Want to talk about it?" he softly asked.

"I'm sorry. I didn't mean for that to happen."

"I'm not. I loved every minute of it."

I grinned sheepishly. "I did too." I snuggled farther in to him. "I spoke with Penny before I came over. It was disturbing. The cold way she looked at me. I felt as though she had crawled inside my mind and twisted everything good, tainting it. I don't know what's going on. This case has got me seriously fucked up. I'm afraid that Gray isn't alive and that her mother really had something to do with her disappearance."

"What makes you think that?"

"She smiled when I told her that I still hadn't found Gray. It was as though she enjoyed the idea of me running around in circles, chasing my tail. Like she knew what had happened to Gray all along."

"Do you really believe that?"

"What other logical explanation is there?"

He sighed. "I don't know, but you can't quit."

"I'm not going to. I will see this to the end. It's just—just so damn confusing."

"Did you find out who is behind the threats?"

I shook my head. "No. I confronted Harold and it's not him."

"How do you know for sure?"

"He all but called me out. Hell, he said that if he wanted to hurt me, he would do it in broad daylight."

"Well, that's a comforting thought."

We both busted out laughing. He really did know how to make me feel better.

"Come on, let's get something to eat. Get your mind off the case for a bit and regroup."

I placed a gentle kiss on his lips. "Thank you."

"My pleasure."

CHAPTER 24

I SAT AT MY DESK AND flipped through the yearbook pages. I used a black permanent marker to cross out every male photo so that I could concentrate strictly on the females. I had taped the computer-generated picture of Gray to the right so I could compare. I had only crossed off two females when Nash dropped a stack of paper on top of the book. I looked up from my task, a tad irritated at him for distracting me.

"What's this?"

"The credit card statements for Penny and Diane. They are from around the time that Gray disappeared. I haven't had time to look through the charges."

"I will do that. All I wanted was the info—I don't have your super connections."

He blasted me with a toothy grin. "Good to know that you still need me around."

I cocked my head to the side, clearly confused by his statement. I was about to ask what the heck he was talking about when he spoke again.

"I cornered Harold outside of the club last night."

My eyebrows rose with burning curiosity. "Seriously?"

"He didn't say much more than what he had already told us but I did get a name from him. Does Brian McCallister ring any bells?"

I thought for a moment, racking my brain. "No. Should it?"

"He is the guy that Penny had an affair with."

"Okay. And what is his significance?"

"Brian McCallister is the chief of police."

"What the fuck does that mean?"

"It means that you have another possible suspect who had many tools at his disposal to get rid of or cover up a crime."

I slapped my hand on my knee. "I'll be damned. How the hell did you get that out of Harold?"

"I can't tell you or I'd have to kill you." He laughed as he strutted out of my office.

"Get in line," I hollered.

I picked up the phone and dialed Omar.

"Good morning," he answered playfully.

"Morning. Hey, I don't want to keep you, but can you tell me about Brian McCallister?"

"The chief of police?" he asked, surprised.

"Yep."

"I don't know him that well. I don't know what I can even tell you about him."

"Is he married, have any kids, know of any affairs that he had eighteen years ago?"

"Seriously, Skye?"

"As a heart attack."

"Fuck, I have no idea. Let me see if I can do some digging. I might know someone I can trust to see if that has any credibility."

"Thank you. I'm sorry to have to put you in the middle of this. I didn't want you a part of it at all but I didn't want to go ask a bunch of questions without some info to help back me up."

"No problem. I will do my best to help you—— you know this."

"Thank you, again."

"You coming over tonight?"

"Not sure yet. Can I let you know later?"

"Sure. Talk to you later."

I hung, energized. No amount of caffeine or nicotine could give me this kind of high.

I set the credit card statements to the side until I finished combing through the yearbook. Two hours later, with my hair sticking up in all directions from pulling on the strands, I had yielded nothing. Not one single female matched the photo. Not even a single facial feature stood out with a likeness. I tossed the books into the garbage can and picked up the statements. I combed through Penny's first. Fifteen minutes later, I shredded the paper. With my yellow highlighter ready, I read through Diane's charges.

"Fuck!" I shouted at the walls of my office. I wanted to throw and break something, anything. There was absolutely no fucking charge on any of their cards that would indicate that they both were involved in her disappearance. They still could be, but not in hiding her away from Harold and the rest of the world. My theory of Gray going to live with Diane was shot down, with no chance of resuscitation.

A soft knock sounded on my door. "Come in."

"I brought you a couple of cookies. Sounded like you needed some comfort."

I beamed up at her. "My savior!"

Her light laughter helped squash the negativity that had surrounded me mere minutes ago. She handed over four peanut butter cookies. I grabbed the plate and stuffed a whole one in my mouth.

I mumbled around the sugary goodness. "So—good."

She laughed her way back to her desk. She was so good to me. The cookies were an excellent substitute for my mother's hugs.

I swiveled my chair back around to face the computer. I typed in Brian McCallister in the search engine. Myriad websites popped up. I clicked on the first one with a profile picture. It was an article commending his son's early rise to stardom on the varsity football team. Low and behold, he went to the same high school as Gray. *Pure coincidence?* Tyler McCallister played his freshman year on the junior varsity team and bumped up to varsity his sophomore year. He had been the star quarterback for the past two years, with colleges knocking on his door. The article was dated six months ago. There was a picture of Brian and his son, posing for the camera.

Despite Gray's brown hair and Tyler's blond hair, they could be twins. They both favored their father. Tyler was tall like his father, where Gray was more petite like her mother. I leaned back in my chair and let out a breath I had been holding. *Holy shit, this could get ugly real quick.* The article mentioned his wife Leslie McCallister and another younger sibling by the name of Marcus. I snatched the last cookie off the plate and rushed to Nash's office.

"Nash, you are never going to believe this shit."

I stopped dead in my tracks as Omar sat in the chair that I usually commandeered. "Omar, I didn't realize that you were here."

"I stopped in to talk to Nash for a moment before I went to see you."

His tone seemed flat and void of the truth. *What the hell was going on?*

"Right. Do you mind waiting for me in my office? I have something that I need to discuss with Nash."

He stood and pecked me on the cheek on his way out.

"It's the office right past Lisa's desk," I said to his back.

I turned around with my arms folded across my chest. "Why was Omar in here?"

I had a feeling that he wasn't actually here to speak with me and that rattled my nerves.

"He was paying me a courtesy visit for one of my other cases. It has nothing to do with the one you're working on. So what brought you in here in such a rush?"

I didn't want to let the conversation go, but what else could I say? If that was all that it was, then I was worrying about nothing. I handed him the article and watched him as he read it. I didn't speak until he set the paper down on his desk.

"It's obvious that Gray is his daughter. I don't need a DNA test to prove what the similarities are showing. He could be behind the calls and vandalism." I was convinced of it.

"I've known him for years and it doesn't add up. He is a fair man and a good officer."

"How does it not add up? He kept his affair with

Penny a secret. What makes you think that he won't go to extreme lengths to keep Gray silent forever? You have to think about the possibility, Nash. Even if you've known the man for years, we are not always what we portray. You, of all people, know that. You even alluded to the fact earlier. Are you going back on your word?"

He threaded his fingers together. "There has to be an explanation to all of this. We need to find out what it is."

"That's exactly what I intend to do. By the way the yearbooks and the credit card statements yielded nothing. Gray is definitely not with Diane."

"Let me speak with Brian. I don't want you near him right now."

I put my hands on my hips and surrendered the speech that I was fully prepared to give. He was right. If Brian was behind the threats, then I needed to be extra cautious. He had the power to dispose of me quickly and quietly. "Let me know what transpires."

"Will do. You better not keep Omar waiting any longer." He scoffed.

"Right." I had completely forgotten that Omar was waiting for me. I turned and went back to my office.

Omar was leaning back in my chair as though he owned the space. I admired his confidence and the way that his uniform fit him like a glove. I had the insane urge to shut and lock the door just so I could have my wicked way with him.

Instead, I leaned against the frame. "You keeping tabs on me at work now?" I joked.

"Nope but I saw an opportunity and grabbed it." He stood and stalked toward me. He grabbed my arm and pulled me tightly to him. He placed his hand on the back of my head and drew me to his lips.

I was so lost in his kiss that I didn't hear anyone approach.

"Briggs," Nash snapped.

I pulled away from Omar and awkwardly turned around to face my boss. The tension ran thick between the two of them.

"I'm taking my girl to lunch. I'll have her back in an hour." Omar winked at Nash.

I watched Nash's jaw muscles work furiously. He was going to blow a gasket and I didn't want to be in the same vicinity when it happened. I mouthed my apologies on the way out. I was the only one who would get hurt during their game of whose dick was bigger. Secretively, I was turned on by the fact that they were both trying to mark me as their territory and yet slightly miffed at their adolescent behavior.

We drove in silence. He picked a fast-food joint. I didn't have an hour to spend at lunch and I knew that he didn't either. He said that to piss Nash off. He handed me the bag of food while he parked the car.

I fished out his and handed it over.

As I unwrapped my chicken sandwich, I asked, "What in the hell possessed you to piss off my boss like that? Nash had a right to snap at me. We were making out at my place of work. That isn't something that I make a habit of."

"Are you pissed that he caught us or pissed that

he witnessed it?"

"Isn't that the same thing?"

"No."

"Look, I don't know what's going on here but Nash is my boss and I need to remain professional while I am at work. I'm glad that you stopped by but kissing will have to wait until I'm off the clock from now on."

"I'm sorry. I don't know what came over me. I guess I was jealous that you two work so closely together and I wanted him to know that you belong to me."

I choked on the bite that I was trying to swallow. "There is nothing going on between Nash and me. There was no need for that little pissing match. What if I had come in to the precinct and started mauling you in front of your coworkers?"

He laughed. "They would enjoy the show. The precinct is pretty dull."

"I'm serious, Omar."

"I know. It won't happen again. But I do see how he looks at you and I don't like it."

"And how is that? Because all I see is annoyance most of the time."

"He looks at you like you are little Red Riding Hood and he is the wolf."

Oh, God, that was freaking hilarious. I laughed until tears squeezed out of the corner of my lids. "Sorry, but that is too funny. Look, I don't want to waste our time arguing about a scenario that isn't even worth talking about. Let's just enjoy lunch, okay?"

"Deal." He took a sip of his soda. "I talked to my dad about Brian."

That piqued my interest. "What did your dad have to say?"

"He wasn't aware of any affair. Pretty much thought that he was one of the good ones. He has a son who is a senior this year and a talented football player. His other son is in middle school. He and his wife have been married for the last twenty years."

I mulled all of that over. He seemed to be the epitome of an exemplary family role model, without a shady background to cover up. I didn't want to discuss anymore with him. It was something that only Nash and I would discuss. Omar and his family didn't belong in the middle of a potential shit storm.

"Thanks for talking with your dad. I hope that it won't go any further than that."

"I'm not telling anyone else, Skye. The potential fallout of those kinds of accusations could be dangerous."

"Exactly. I don't want to see you or your family hurt from what I uncover."

He dropped me back off at the office. "Will I see you later?"

I leaned in the open passenger window. "Probably not. I've got a lot of work to get done tonight. I'm sorry. How about tomorrow?"

"Sounds good. Bye."

I waved and turned to go in to the building. I knew as soon as my foot hit the top of the landing, Nash would call out to me.

CHAPTER 25

*S*URE ENOUGH!

"Briggs!" Nash hollered.

I sent a knowing look to Lisa before I opened his door. She smiled back sympathetically. I shut it behind me to minimize what the rest of the team could hear.

"Hey, boss. What's up?" I asked innocently.

"Tell your boyfriend that we are not running a brothel here."

I gasped at the underlying meaning of his harsh words. "I'm not a whore, Nash. Damn it, we were only kissing, for Christ's sake."

"I didn't call you a whore," he barked.

"You implied that I was."

He ran his hand through his hair. "Make out with him somewhere else. Not on company time. You got it?" he seethed.

"No problem. I told him as much when we were at lunch. It won't happen again."

I could visibly see the tension release from his shoulders. "I've got a meeting set up with Brian at the end of the week. Stay out of trouble until then. Leave Penny and Harold alone until after I've talked with him. You can work on your other cases."

"Got it. Anything else?"

"No."

"Good. I've got some calls to make."

I stormed out of his office. I wanted to throttle him. He had no right to insinuate that I was some kind of floozy. I had never brought my love life to work until today. In the span of a minute, Omar had managed to put a crack in the foundation that I had worked so hard to build. I was pissed off at the both of them.

I slumped into my chair, not sure what to do with myself. I had to put Gray's case on hold for the time being. I wasn't thrilled about it but once again, Nash had made perfect sense.

"Don't worry about Nash. He has been in a testy mood these last couple of weeks. I have to admit that your little make-out session was pretty hot and heavy. Ryker, Lisa, and I had placed bets on what base you were going to get to." Hawke walked in and sat on the corner of my desk as though he had done it every day.

"Ha! Who won the bet?"

He grinned. "I did."

"How much you win?"

"Forty bucks."

"Nice. You treating me to dinner with your winnings?"

"I think you got enough man trouble without throwing me into the mix." He laughed as though his joke was hilarious.

I ignored his last dig. "Where you been? I haven't seen you around here lately."

"Out of town. Had some things to take care of."

He was being evasive. I wondered what case he

had been working. "You back for a bit?"

"Yeah."

Okay, this was strange. All I have ever had with Hawke was a one-sided conversation. I would talk about random shit and he would grunt back. I wondered what was up with Chatty-Cathy today.

"I wanted to tell you to watch your back with Brian McCallister. I've dealt with him enough over the years and let's just say that he is a bit hairy at the heel. I don't trust him as far as I can throw him."

"Nash told me the opposite about him. Said he was a stand up guy."

He shrugged with indifference. "Regardless, do not trust anyone but who is in this office. That includes your boyfriend. We protect our own. I'm sure Nash has his reasons for what he said, as do I."

"Thanks." I swallowed hard, trying to manage the feeble answer.

He left my office just as quickly as he had entered. Today was a day for strange things. I'd have to look on the calendar to see whether it was a full moon. I dialed the five clients who wanted their spouses followed. I filled up tomorrow with in-house meetings. These should take me all the way up to when Nash talked with Brain. After these, I would be back to working Gray's case full-time. I wanted it finished, one way or another.

I called out to whoever was listening. "I'm going home. See you in the morning."

The drive home was quick and easy to navigate. All I wanted to do was crawl under the covers and sleep. I headed up the walkway, fishing for my phone so I could use the flashlight to insert my key. I really needed to install a motion light. It would make this painful process so much easier. I found it and flipped it on. I made the motions to insert the key, when the door inched open with barely a touch.

Shit. Do I go in or call the police? I made a mad dash back to my car and dialed the emergency operator with trembling fingers and reported the break-in. It was impossible to steady my erratic pulse. I stayed on the line as she requested and waited until I saw the blue and red flashing lights. I stayed in my car until I was approached. The officer knocked on my window and I powered it down.

"Are you the one who called in the break-in?"

"Yes, sir. I am the one," I answered more confidently now that the cavalry had arrived.

I noticed another cop car slam on its brakes out in front of my house. The door slammed shut and I could hear the heavy pounding of work boots.

"I've got this, Mike," Omar said in an authoritative voice.

I opened my door and stepped out of my car. "Hi, sorry we are meeting like this."

My mind was a crazy mixture of hope and fear.

He pulled me into a tight hug and rubbed his strong hands up and down my back. "I wish you would've called me first."

"Isn't that breaking some kind of protocol?" I tried to make it sound like a joke.

"No. I would've called it in and I wouldn't have been scared out of my mind worrying that something had happened to you as I raced to get here."

"I'm really sorry, Omar. I wasn't thinking straight. I didn't even go in—just went back to my car and made the call."

"Shh, *mi reina*. It's going to be okay. I'll stay right here while the other guys go in."

"Thank you."

I stood in his arms, soaking up his warmth and strength. I was exactly where I wanted to be. Well, maybe inside my own home without the knowledge that someone had broken in and robbed me of what little security I had left. I didn't know what kind of damage I was going to walk into but I felt unclean. It was a violating emotion to know that your personal things had been gone through and possibly destroyed. *How was I ever going to enjoy the sanctity of my home again?*

"Ma'am?"

I stepped away from my security blanket and faced the officer Omar had called Mike.

"Yes?" I quivered with fear, anticipating what he was about to tell me.

"You are all set to go in and make sure that nothing was stolen. We've already fingerprinted so you are free to touch any surface."

I nodded and straightened my spine, preparing for the potential disastrous scene.

"Omar, I've got Skye. You can go back to your shift," Nash all but commanded him.

I was so engrossed in trying to drum up enough poise that I didn't hear him approach.

I angled my body toward Omar. "It's okay. You need to get back to work before you get in trouble. I know you're on the clock. I'll call you in a bit."

I placed a chaste kiss on his cheek. I didn't have the energy to watch them fight. At the moment, I didn't care who was with me when I went through my house. I just wanted to grab a bag and get the hell out of here. Until I got new locks and a security system in place, I would be staying at the office or...fuck, I would think about it later.

"You can stay with me tonight. Nash can drop you off at the precinct when you are done."

"Thanks."

I walked away from the both of them, but before I could enter the home by myself, I could feel Nash standing next to me. He placed his hand on my shoulder, grounding me. His fingers feathered down my arm until they reached mine. He threaded his thick fingers through my smaller ones and infused his strength into my soul.

"Ready?" His voice was soft and supportive.

"I think so." I looked over at him with trepidation.

"I won't leave your side. I will hold your hand the whole time, if you need me to. Or I can go in and grab what you want for you."

"No. I want to do this. Just help me get through the door first. I need you to do that because I don't think that I can step over that threshold without you."

I know I sounded needy and if Omar had been there to witness our exchange, he would have every right to be jealous or hate me forever. However, I wasn't trying to be romantic or get Nash in my bed. For this one time, I needed his hand to hold, and his friendship to help me get through this. If I couldn't have Jackie here, Nash was the next best thing.

He walked through the door first and pulled me along after him. He knew that I would stay frozen to that very spot if he didn't give me a nudge. Before I had called the cops, the house was pitch-black; now it erupted in a blaze of light. I knew that the cops had searched every nook and cranny for a body to associate to the crime and it had resulted in only empty space. However, it was difficult to imagine that the perpetrator was already gone. I had the uneasy feeling that they were hiding in wait.

I walked behind him, with only inches separating us. I didn't look up, only down at my feet, matching his steps.

"Get your timid ass out from behind me, Briggs." He spoke with an authoritative air.

I stepped around him, ready to kick his ass. "What the hell, Nash. You are supposed to be on my side."

"I am and I'll be damned if you hide. You are stronger than that. This will not be your breaking point. Look up and look around at the destruction. Use it to fuel your anger."

I grinned at him. He was such an ass and I completely fell for his reverse psychology. "Why do you always have to be right?" His boyish smile charmed my heart, but only a tiny bit. "Let's do this."

He took his index finger and lifted my chin. "That's my girl."

I toured my home with a detached eye. I would not allow the harsh words spray-painted on the walls crumble my psyche. Dishes were broken, my clothes thrown haphazardly, but what hurt the most was the destruction to my reading nook. They had taken a knife and slashed my favorite cushions to shreds. Pages of my favorite hardback books were torn out and littered the floor. I bent to pick up the pages and felt my composure begin to crumble. I didn't care about the other stuff; it was replaceable. However, those books were all given to me throughout my lifetime from my mother. Some of them had been signed with a loving message that I would never be able to get back. Those words were forever lost. My heart hurt; tiny prickles of pain cracked the large muscle. I wanted to howl with rage and sadness. Nash came up behind me and helped me stand. With the torn paper still gripped in my hand, he pulled me to his chest. I whimpered and then let the rush of tears pour down my face and soak his shirt. After I had shed all the tears that my body could summon, I lifted my head from his chest.

"I'm sorry about your shirt," I commented dryly, not at all sorry––more embarrassed that he had watched my breakdown.

"I'm not." He held me tightly.

"Why would they do this? I can handle everything else. But my books––why?" I begged him for a logical answer.

"Because they were what you loved the most. Whoever is behind this wanted you to hurt so terribly that you would give up."

I steeled my back and stepped from his comforting arms. "They've got another thing coming if they think that this would make me quit. They simply managed to piss me off more. I want them to hurt."

His jaw muscles worked overtime before a sinister grin formed from his beautiful lips. "And so they shall."

CHAPTER 26

I STEPPED OUT OF THE CAR and leaned back in before I shut the door "Thanks for dropping me off. I'll see you at the office in the morning."

"If you want to take the day off, I understand."

He threw me a lifeline in case I needed to lick my wounds. I shook my head. "No, but thanks. I've got some meetings set up."

"See you in the morning."

I nodded and shut the door. I walked through the precinct's doors and informed the front desk that I was here to wait for Omar. I sat on the most uncomfortable bench and waited. After an hour, my butt ached. I stood and stretched, working out the kinks. Omar walked through the bullpen and toward me.

"I hope you weren't waiting long?" He placed his hand through mine. "Are you ready to go home?"

Home? Was Omar's my house of refuge or truly my home? I couldn't think about anything more than tonight. For this one night, I would allow him to call it my home as well. "Yes."

I carried my overnight bag to his bedroom and released a pent-up breath. My soul was tired and disillusioned. I looked over my shoulder when I heard him walk in.

"Are you hungry?" he asked.

"No. If you don't mind, I just want to shower and sleep."

"Not at all."

I went to his bathroom and grabbed a quick shower. I'm glad that he hadn't offered to join me. I let the warm water cleanse my soul. I stood under the spray of water until it ran cold. He was already in bed by the time that I had walked out of the steaming bathroom. He lay naked from the waist up, outstretching his arm for me to climb in next to him. I pulled the covers back and hopped in. I scooted until I was enveloped in his scent and warmth.

He placed a kiss to my forehead. "Sleep, *mi reina.*"

A gentle smile touched my lips. I closed my eyes and let the heaviness of sleep take me under.

I woke to a tender tweak of my nipples through the oversized shirt that I had worn to bed the previous night. My thighs clenched as heat pulled into my core. I arched my back as he massaged my breasts. His fingers danced their way down my stomach and under my panties. I opened for his greedy fingers. They expertly rubbed my clit while he placed kisses along my neck. I moaned as he drew my pending orgasm closer. He flipped me on to my stomach and covered my back with his hard body. He pushed the shirt up, exposing my barely covered ass. His fingers slipped along the thin waistband of my underwear and pulled them skillfully down my legs.

"I love your ass, *mi reina.* It's gorgeous."

I squirmed from his words. I was worked up from his fingers and wanted him inside me. I brought my knees up under me, and leaned my upper torso on to the bed. I was open for the taking. My pussy was wet and ready for his thick shaft to take me to an orgasmic finale.

He put his mouth on my clit and licked his way back. "You fucking taste amazing."

"Please, Omar, fuck me."

The tip of his dick replaced his tongue at my entrance, and then slammed home. I lifted my head off the mattress and moaned in ecstasy. His hips thrust, making my pussy wet for every stroke that he would give me. He placed his thumb along the tight muscle of my asshole. I immediately clenched, curious but also scared to have my back end fucked.

"Just my thumb, relax. You'll love it."

I relaxed and let him fondle my virgin area. Once I let go of the worry, it felt fantastic. His thumb slightly pushed in and my body thrashed from the double onslaught.

"Oh, God. I'm going to come," I shouted.

"Yes, I want to feel you come on my cock."

He reached his other hand to my clit and I was done. I screamed in ecstasy. He hit every erogenous button that I didn't know I had even possessed. I had come apart at the seams. He released a grunt and spilled his seed as my pussy milked him.

He rolled off, taking me with him. I lay upon his chest and kissed him. "Best wake-up of all time!"

My body bounced as he chuckled. "Want some breakfast before you go to the office?"

"That sounds perfect."

He gave me another kiss to remember. "Now, you need to get off me so that I can make this so-called perfect breakfast."

I lightly swatted him and moved away. "I'm gonna hop in your shower and get ready, if you don't mind."

"You are welcome to anything in my home."

I smiled and made a dash to the bathroom. I let the pulsating stream ease the tension of my muscles. I was bound and determined to push last night's events behind me.

Work was exactly what I needed. I submerged myself in the five new clients who had hired me to tail their partners. I received all of their schedules, the times, and days that their partners were supposed to be working or traveling. They did most of the legwork for me and still paid me the retainer to start the tails. I loved it when things went smoothly.

A knock sounded on my office door. I looked over at the entryway and raised my eyebrows. "Since when do you ever knock on my door? Hell, Nash, it's already opened, for goodness' sake."

His chuckle brightened my day even more. "We all deserve a little courtesy once in a while."

I laughed at him. "Sure, boss. What's up?"

"I'm heading out to talk with Brian. We have a lunch meeting. I'll come back to the office and let you know what transpired."

"Thanks. I'm going to stick around here until

you get back. I don't have anything pressing today. I've got five new clients to work background checks on and start compiling more information."

"I'll be back before three."

"Sounds good. Thanks."

I grabbed my phone to look at the incoming text that chimed while I was talking with Nash.

Have an hour free. Want to grab lunch?

My fingers flew over the small keys. I wasn't going to let this opportunity pass. Jackie hardly ever had a free lunch; she usually worked through them.

Absolutely. Meet you at Shauny's in fifteen? I'm on my way.

Shauny's was a diamond in the rough. It was a quaint little hole in the wall. They served the best sub sandwiches around. My mouth watered just thinking about the Italian sub with a side of thick steak fries that I always ordered. Everything was pretty good but the Italian was my favorite. Its flavor never disappointed.

I picked a booth in the back. I faced the door and waited for Jackie to enter. I had ordered our drinks minutes before she had arrived.

"Girl, this job is going to kill me and I'm not sleeping enough." She sighed as she slid into the booth.

I chuckled at her aggravation. Even when she was tired and stressed, she looked magnificent. "When do the owners get back in town?"

"In a week. When it's all said and done, I'm going to sleep for a month."

I rolled my eyes at her. "No, you're not. You'll jump right back in with your next project. Sleep is overrated and you know it."

"Damn, I hate it when you're right. Did you order our subs, too, or just the drinks?"

"Just the drinks. I never know what sub you are going to choose. The waiter should be over in a minute to finish taking our order."

"Thank fuck. I'm starving."

"You're always hungry and I don't know where you put it. I'm so damn jealous of you right now. It'll take me months to work off these calories."

She winked. "Shut up! You need to give me Hawke's digits."

My mouth hung open in surprise. Her comment rendered me speechless. She made comments about bedding the guys all the time but I didn't think that she was serious about it.

She took a long pull of her diet soda. "I'm serious. He is sex on a stick and I want a piece of that action."

"You really are serious, aren't you?" I couldn't help my surprise.

"Yes and you know it. Girl, I want no-strings, hot and sweaty monkey sex."

I cupped my hands over my ears and sang *la-la-la*.

She grabbed my wrists, chuckling. "Quit being the prude that I know damn well you aren't. Give me his number or I'll show up at the office and make a scene that's going to totally embarrass you."

I shook my head. "All right. All right." I picked up my phone and scrolled through my contacts. It could go either way. Hawke would either be pissed as fuck at me for giving out his number or thanking the sex gods that I practically hand-delivered one of the most beautiful women in the world to him. I rattled off the number to her and then set it back down on the table.

She gobbled the number up and quickly stored it in her cell before it disappeared forever. I couldn't help but shake my head and chuckle at her.

It didn't take the waiter long to put in our order. We finished our lunch in record time, hating that we couldn't extend our visit. There was still so much that we needed to catch up on. We said our good-byes with the promise of seeing each other again soon.

I took the stairs two at a time and ran the rest of the way to my office and waited for Nash to get back. My concentration was shot. All I could think about was the conversation that Nash was having with Brian. *Would he tell Nash the truth?* Hawke alluded that Brian wasn't a guy to be trusted. On the other hand, Nash reported the opposite. If Brian had anything to do with Gray's disappearance, I highly doubted that he would confess his sins to Nash over lunch.

I glanced at the clock on the wall. The hands moved at a snail's pace around the face of the clock. I had another hour to kill before he would return. I stared vacantly at the white painted wall, twiddling my thumbs, and mentally urged the time to speed up.

"Briggs! Get in my office," Nash barked.

I jumped out of the chair as if my ass were on fire. I shot through the doorway, speed walking the short distance toward his office. I turned and closed the door silently as I stepped through. I walked brusquely toward my favorite chair, plopped down, and braced myself for what was to come. My leg bounced in tune with the way my teeth gnawed at my already short fingernails.

"Brian does not have any interaction with the McCullums."

I dropped my hand on the armrest and leaned forward. "What do you mean––that he does not know them? Gray could be his son's twin, that's how much they look alike."

"Lucky for you, I grabbed his napkin that he used for lunch. As we speak, my guy is running his DNA."

I relaxed slightly.

"It will only confirm what he has already told me."

I tensed. "Nash, how can you believe what he says with such utter conviction?"

"The reasons don't matter. It is the truth. You need to find another angle. I will give you the results of the test when it comes back."

I stomped back to my office. I had heard enough. I was fucking sick to death of dead ends. I hadn't completely nixed Brian as a possible suspect. Hope raged against the doubts that clouded my mind.

I sifted through my thoughts. Harold was a wife-beating bastard who claimed Gray was not his daughter. He claimed that Penny had had an affair that resulted in Gray. He didn't visit his family and never spoke of them to outsiders. He was a workaholic who spent his free time playing cards at the country club. His landscaping business took off and was extremely profitable.

Penny and Gray led an extremely sheltered life. Penny had minimal help raising her daughter.

Her sister had offered to help them disappear and create a new life but Penny had refused. Penny had no other family and was estranged from the only one who tried to help. She volunteered at the school library but had no other job outside of the home. She had no friends and, other than her brief affair, only socialized with her husband. However, the affair in question didn't happen, according to the accused party.

Gray was an excellent student. She had remained close with her grandparents, unbeknownst to her father. Which seemed to be the only thing that she did that was against the rules. She didn't have a regular teenage life or friends outside of school. She had no known boyfriend and stayed out of trouble.

What was I missing? Based on their family dynamics, it stood to reason that Harold had done something with or to his daughter. He had despised her from the beginning. Penny's affair had started the chain of events that had led to Gray's disappearance. The mother treasured and protected her daughter; would she hurt her? *Who was behind the vandalism? Why trash my house? What was the purpose of those threatening calls?* A multitude of questions with no clear answers.

"DNA results came back."

Nash slammed the paperwork on my desk.

I didn't bother to even pick them up. I trusted that he had already combed through the results. *Damn it, could this case get any more fucked up?*

"I'm going home. I need to reboot or slam my head against the wall. I'm not sure which." I stood to leave but Nash blocked my way.

"Give me another hour and then I'll drive you home."

I cocked my head to the side and raised my eyebrow. "Whatever for?"

"For once, just do what I ask. Please."

It was the please that did it. I sat back in my chair. "All right. You've got one hour and I'm heading home. I can drive myself, thank you very much."

"Fine but don't leave for at least an hour."

I rolled my eyes and laughed silently to myself as his sigh of frustration followed him down the hall.

I futzed around the office, mostly rearranging my files, putting them in order of importance. Gray's file remained open and on my desk, the papers no longer in any kind of order. I wouldn't file it until I had officially closed it. I glanced at the clock. It had been exactly one hour. I snatched my purse and headed home.

Nervousness twisted in my gut as I put the car in park. Ready or not, I had to face my home. It was time to stop hiding and put it back together. I suspended my forward momentum for a minute before I was able to straighten my spine and face the mess that waited for me inside. Before I could unlock the door, Nash pulled in behind my car.

He stepped out of his vehicle, leaving it running. "I told you to wait for me."

I swiveled on my heels. "And I told you that I was going by myself."

"You need the alarm code."

"What did you do?" I placed my hands on my hips.

"Go ahead and unlock the door. I'll enter the code as soon as we walk through. You can type it in your phone so you don't forget."

The beeping noise from the alarm immediately warned us of our entry. Nash stealthily entered the four-digit number and the annoying warning quit as the robotic voice told us that the system was disarmed. I released a breath that I hadn't even realized that I had been holding in.

"Thank you."

"I'll show you how to use it in a minute."

I nodded and set my purse on the kitchen counter. I looked around and took in my surroundings. My mouth hung open from the shock of a clean house. I walked through my home as though I were in a trance. Everything that had been damaged had been fixed. All of my broken items had been replaced. It was as though nothing had ever happened. I walked back toward the kitchen.

"Jack, the boys, and I came over yesterday and put it all back together. We didn't want you to come back here and have to deal with it on your own."

I rushed into his arms. I stayed in the comfort and safety of his warm body until my tears subsided. It could have been for hours but he didn't seem to mind. He held me and let me cry until I pulled back.

"Thank-you seems like such a small thing to say for all that you guys have done for me." I hiccupped.

He pulled me back to his chest and wrapped his strong arms around me. He placed his arm behind my knees and lifted me as though I were merely a child and carried me to the couch. He sat down and continued to cradle me in his lap. "Shh."

His fingers combed through my hair soothingly. He gently placed his full lips to my forehead. It was the sweetest gesture that I'd ever experienced. My body hummed with desire and the need to have his lips cover mine. I was with Omar and this was not the time or place to give my body permission to have its way with Nash. So, I snuggled deeper into his lap.

"Nash, what comes next?"

"I don't know." He sighed and resumed massaging my scalp. "Do you want me to stay with you tonight?"

Yes! "No, thank you. You guys have done such a wonderful job erasing the damage. It will take time for my mind to forget but I need to do that on my own. I can't afford to continue to hide." I burrowed deeper, not wanting him to let me go just yet. "Would you stay a little while longer?" I mumbled into his chest.

I was afraid to look up at him. I didn't want him to leave and yet I was scared that I would do something stupid the longer he held on to me.

"I'll stay as long as you like." His lips brushed the crown of my head.

I smiled contently and relished being held.

CHAPTER 27

NASH LEFT SOMETIME AROUND MID-NIGHT. I watched him maneuver his car out of my drive. When I could no longer see his taillights, I backed away from the door and grabbed a glass of wine. My stomach was tied in knots. I wanted to be brave but my insides were clawing their way up my throat. I felt as though I were in a glass house, trapped and being watched. I had set the alarm right after Nash had walked out the door. Logically, I knew that I was safe but the irrational fear had already rooted itself in the dark recesses of my mind, constantly trying to gain control. The more wine I poured down my throat, the more I found a semblance of peace.

I left all the lights blazing as I stumbled to my room. I dragged my purse and set it on my nightstand. I felt some comfort knowing that my gun was close by. In my inebriated state, I hadn't thought to remove it from my purse. I passed out, semi-conscious of the danger that lurked near me.

The pounding at my temples woke me the next morning. I stumbled out of bed and rummaged through my medicine cabinet for some aspirin to kill the little trolls that knocked around my skull.

After I had gotten ready, I checked my phone. I

sent a text to Nash and then Omar. I wasn't ready to have a conversation with either of them. I knew Jack wouldn't pick up her phone so I called her quickly and left her a message, thanking her for cleaning up my house. I grabbed my keys, set the alarm, and got in my car.

I felt the cold metal of the pistol against my temple. My skin was already sensitive from my hangover. The steel of the barrel sent a ripple of pain across my forehead. I winced. Slowly and methodically, I moved my hand toward my purse nestled on the passenger seat.

"Don't move."

I immediately stopped my hand and drew it back to the steering wheel. I looked into the mirror, trying to identify my kidnapper. They stayed half hidden behind my seat and what I could see was completely covered. The voice was muffled from the knitted mask that they wore. I couldn't decipher whether they were male or female.

"What do you want?" I tried to hide the quiver in my voice but failed miserably.

"Not so damn confident now, are you?" Their words twisted with anger.

I remained quiet, thinking of a way out of this.

"Back out and go north. Do as I say and I won't hurt you."

Those exact words were printed in the Kidnapper's 101 handbook. In reality, this was where my life was going to end. A bead of sweat trickled down the side of my forehead and landed in my ear. *How the hell was I going to get out of this?* They made it look so easy on TV. I backed the car out like I was told and headed north. I thought about pushing down the pedal and slamming on my brakes. My seat belt was on and I just might be able to knock the person around enough for me to escape. I shook that thought away. I had nowhere to run to. I would be like a deer out in the open, ripe for the killing.

About halfway out of town, I was instructed to pull in to a deserted gas station. I put the car in park with a plan in place. I pushed the button and unclicked my seatbelt. I made a grab for the handle when I felt a cloth cover my mouth. Instinctively I knew I had to hold my breath. I held it for so long that my lungs burned with the need to draw in a breath. I clutched at the arm around my neck, holding me in place, while my other hand scratched and pawed at the immovable hand holding tightly to the rag over my mouth. My lungs convulsed and I gave in, greedily breathing in the odorless concoction that would put me to sleep. My body instantly sagged and gave in to my kidnapper.

CHAPTER 28

I ROLLED MY HEAD TO THE side, waiting for my stomach to empty what little contents it had stored from the previous night. I gagged and dry heaved without an ounce of relief. All that empty retching only brought my head to screaming levels of pain. I desperately wanted a drink of water to soothe my dry mouth and some aspirin for this headache that threatened to split my skull in half.

My vision cleared and I was able to look around at the room I was being held in. It was dark, void of any windows, and smelled of moldy earth. I rocked my way to a sitting position. My wrists were bound tightly behind my back, which made any kind of normal movement extremely difficult. Thank God for small miracles that my feet were free.

I wasn't aware of what time it was or what day. I couldn't have been out for more than a couple of hours but I could've been drugged with something else while I was passed out. I moved my lower body, contorting into a position that only gymnasts and devout yoga individuals could perform easily. I shimmied my lower half through the circle my arms had made until they were no longer behind but now bound in front. They maybe tied but I could still hit with enough force to inflict damage.

A door opened and light flooded the small enclosure. I blinked rapidly, adjusting to the brightness. A wooden stairwell off to my right led to the only escape route. My breaths came in pants as I waited for my captor to reveal him or herself. I held my breath with each creak of a step. My kidnapper stood before me with a gun pointed at my heart. I released my breath slowly, making sure I hadn't moved a muscle.

The black-clad figure continued to wear a mask. Their clothing was baggy and I couldn't gage what gender they were. The mask covered their head; only their eyes poked out at me.

"What do you want from me?"

"You'll find out soon enough." His or her voice was muffled by the knit cap that covered their mouth.

"How long have I been down here?" I asked somewhat breathlessly.

"Not long enough. No one will find you and there is no escape."

Why was I being toyed with? If they wanted me dead, why not kill me as soon as I sat behind the wheel? What was the purpose of bringing me here alive? Panic bubbled beneath the surface. *Torture. Shit, anything but that.*

I hadn't noticed it before but they held a glass of water in the hand not occupying the gun. *Keep me alive long enough to slowly kill me. What a pleasant thought that was!* I waited in silence for them to speak more. He or she put the glass down by a steel beam in the middle of the room and then turned and walked up the stairs backward, keeping the gun trained on me the whole time. I continued to sit in the same position as I had when they had come down, long after the door was shut.

I was thirsty and wanted to drink that glass of water. *But was it poisoned?* I wasn't that desperate; I didn't drink from it but I looked at it longingly.

CHAPTER 29

SKYE SHOULD'VE BEEN TO WORK by now. It had been over an hour since her text, telling me that she was fine and on her way. I looked at my watch for the millionth time in the last five minutes. I continued to pace my office, swearing under my breath. Did she stop off to meet up with her *boyfriend?* I loathed that man. I did a thorough background check on him. He was an excellent officer, albeit young, who had nothing but good things said about him. I had worked with him a handful of times on some of my cases and found him knowledgeable and good at his job. Yet, I still hated him.

He was the one she shared her bed with. He was allowed to touch her lithe body. I could only dream of her. The small taste I'd had had done nothing but increase the burning desire that surged through my body. It didn't matter whether she was standing next to me or miles away; I wanted her. She dominated my thoughts to the point that she owned me. I couldn't allow her to get that close to me. If I had, I would destroy her innocence. I had lived a life full of dark secrets, ones that I wouldn't taint her beauty with. Ryker and Hawke knew what they were only because we had lived through them together. My brothers-in-arms were almost as dangerous as I was.

"Lisa, have you talked to Skye recently?" I barked through the door.

"No, not this morning. Is everything all right?"

"Yes. I was just curious."

At least I hoped everything was okay. I stalked to the door and closed it carefully as to not let Lisa think that I was upset. The less she knew, the better. I pulled my cell phone out of my pocket and dialed Omar's number.

"Have you heard from Skye this morning?" I growled into the mouthpiece.

"Why?"

"Just answer the fucking question. I don't have time for this shit."

"I got a text from her this morning, saying that she was going to work and would call me later. Is she okay?" His tone was one of affection and worry.

I never wanted to punch someone so bad in my entire life. I unclenched my fist, trying to dislodge the jealousy that had balled tightly around my limbs. I hung up the phone, tempted to chuck it across the room. I knew he would call me again but I had to get myself under control before I could talk to him.

I let it go to voicemail before I hit his number again.

"Had another call I had to take. As far as I know, she is okay. I wanted to check because she hadn't come to the office yet. I thought that maybe she had stayed with you last night."

Lies, all lies. I knew that she stayed home because

I was with her until late. I practically begged her to let me stay with her. I would've been a perfect gentleman and slept on her couch even though I wanted desperately to be in her bed with her underneath me.

"No. She never returned my calls last night. I figured that she was home and putting it back together."

Asshole! If he had truly loved her, then he would've enlisted us to put it back together for her so she wouldn't have had to face that alone. Instead, her true friends worked all day and night to get it back in order while he spent the night fucking her. God, I could kill him myself.

"We took care of that for her. I followed her home last night to make sure that she knew how to operate the alarm system. I left once she seemed comfortable."

"Fuck, I didn't even think about that. Why didn't you call me to help?" he accused me.

"I've got to go. Call me if you hear anything."

"Do the same."

"Yep."

I hung up on him again. *Fuck him.* I wasn't going to tell him shit but I certainly expected him to inform me if he heard from her. He was the type of guy who would. However, I was not.

I looked at my watch again and ground my teeth together. I sent her another text. I stared at the delivered but not read message for a good fifteen minutes before I rang her phone. It went straight to voicemail. *Damn it, where the fuck was she?*

"Lisa, would you holler to Ryker and Hawke and tell them to get their ass in my office and pronto," I shouted into the intercom.

I'm sure they heard me loud and clear from their office. Lisa didn't even respond to my request; she could hear the urgency in my voice. Not even a minute later, they were stood at attention before me.

"I don't have any proof but my gut tells me that Skye is in trouble."

They both trusted me with their lives. They nodded their heads in unison.

"Where do you want us to start?" Ryker asked.

"Ryker, you head to her house. Hawke, you pay a visit to Jack. Check back in as soon as you get any information."

They ran out the door, swiftly and deadly. I trusted that they would leave no stone unturned.

"What can I do?" Lisa had poked her head around the doorframe.

I could see the worry radiating off her.

"Keep the phone lines open and if you would stay a little later tonight..."

"Not a problem. I'll let my husband know what's going on. If there is anything else that we can do, please let me know."

"Thank you. That is all for now."

I could count on one hand the people who I could trust. My team encompassed most of them.

"Lisa, I'm heading out. I've got my cell—call me with anything. I don't care how insignificant it might be. I'll check back with you in a bit."

"I will."

I nodded. The mother in her wouldn't rest until we had found Skye. She had already become such a strong team player in the little time that she had come on board. She would fight tooth and nail for all of us. We had become her second family and we would reciprocate if the need arose.

Every minute that the clock ticked, Skye's life became more perilous.

CHAPTER 30

I LICKED MY DRY LIPS. I continued to study the damn glass of water. It taunted me, calling out for me to take a long, satisfying gulp. Over the last couple of hours, I had steadily inched my way toward the clear liquid. I hadn't consciously realized it until I sat within arm's reach.

I hadn't seen my captor in some time and for that I was thankful. Just as I was about to reach for the soothing liquid, the door opened and the room flooded with warm light. I had grown accustomed to the darkness and the fluorescent of the bulb felt as though I were looking directly at the sun. I squinted until a shadow loomed over me. I looked up at the same dark-clad figure towering over me. The urge to scoot back pressed along my spinal cord. I stayed where I was and ignored all of the warnings that my brain shouted, to move as far away as I could.

A black-booted foot rose at the knee, extending right toward my face. I couldn't move my body in time but I was able to lean to the right. The foot connected with my left clavicle. The kick struck the bone with enough force that my shoulder slumped and a white-hot pain shot through my arm. I curled into a tight ball to protect my shoulder. I tried not to whimper but the pain was so intense.

"Get up, bitch."

I could feel the nasty spittle that sprayed out of their mouth and onto my neck. I cringed and shrunk into myself tighter.

A swift kick to my ribs moved me about an inch from where I had lain. *Fuck, that hurt.* I would continue to take it until I could assess the damage and find a way out of this hellhole, or at least die trying. My body hurt and I was exhausted but I would not fight back yet. It was necessary to conserve my energy until the last possible moment. I had no grand illusion that Nash or Omar would come to my rescue. It was on me to save myself. I had to take whatever punishment my captor felt that I needed to endure until they revealed their identity.

The punishing kicks continued until I could hear panting from their exertion. Slowly the kicks lost their potency and died down altogether. I lay there and listened to their retreating footsteps. It wasn't until the room was encased in darkness that I moved my body tenderly to a sitting position. The pain from my shoulder had lessened. I was able to keep my arm tight against my body to help further ease the stabbing-like feeling. I gently probed my ribs with my bad arm. Nothing was broken but they were bruised.

Fuck. I was a mess. I wouldn't last long if I didn't fight back. I scooted to the water and drank the glass dry. It did nothing to soothe my parched throat. I instantly craved more. I slumped against the steel beam, tilted my head back, and closed my eyes.

CHAPTER 31

I SPED ALONG THE QUIET STREETS of our town. I skidded into a parking spot in front of McCullum's Landscaping. I threw the truck in park and jumped out before the tires had a chance to catch up to the brakes. I swung the door open and stomped toward the receptionist's desk. She was a petite woman in her early forties. I didn't know her name nor did I introduce myself.

"Where is Harold?" I threw the words at her like stones.

"Is he expecting you?" Her temper flared.

"Yes. He was supposed to meet me a half an hour ago. He never made it." I toned down my anger, trying to get on her good side.

"He is probably running late from the jobsite this morning. I can give him a call for you." She stirred uneasily in her chair.

I inhaled large quantities of air through my nostrils and exhaled them at the slowest rate I could manage. When I felt more in control, I answered her.

"Could you please tell me where he is working this morning? I'm a private investigator and I desperately need his help." My response held only minor annoyance.

I was hoping that by telling a smidgen of truth, she would tell me where he was.

She bit down on her lip and looked away.

"Please, miss. I need his help," I begged helplessly.

She was the key to finding him quickly. I could search the city, it wasn't that big, but I would be wasting precious time.

"He is in the River Oak community. Four-seventy-eight Riverside Drive."

"Thank you," I barely managed to get out as I ran to my car.

The house was easy to find. I pulled up to the curb slowly as to not garner his attention. Simply a normal day in the neighborhood.

I stalked toward my prey. He never heard my silent steps as I drew near. I grabbed the back of his neck, hauled him up off his feet, and slammed him onto his back, down to the unforgiving ground. His breath made a whooshing sound as the impact knocked the breath out of him. He looked up at me with wide, terror-filled eyes. I grinned sadistically down at him. He had no clue as to all of the sick and twisted ways that I would torture him. I wanted to make him hurt and if Skye didn't make it, he would pray for death before I finished him.

"Where the fuck is Skye?" I gritted through my teeth, barely controlling the anger that rolled through my blood.

"I——I don't know what you are talking about," he stuttered.

"I'm only going to ask you one more time. Where is Skye?" I enunciated each word.

He pawed at the hand I had wrapped around his neck. If I didn't let up soon, his source of air would be cut off.

"I don't know. I didn't do anything to her. I swear," his voice screeched.

I removed my hand from around his neck and allowed him to gasp for air. I had replaced my hand with a heavily booted foot on his chest.

"Harold. Now is not the time to lie to me. Skye is missing and I know that you know where she is."

"I'm telling you the truth, I swear it. I don't know where she is" He shook violently.

I looked down. The front of his pants was soaked. I chuckled demonically to myself. I'd been tortured in a multitude of fashions and had yet to piss myself. I shook my head with disgust. I took my foot off him and hauled him to his feet.

"You better start fucking talking or I swear you'll lose all of your bodily functions before I'm through with you." My eyes hardened along with my voice.

Another stream of piss flowed down his trousers. "Follow me back to my office and I will tell you everything that I know."

I shook my head. "Nope. We will do this right here and right now. I don't have the time to waste." I pushed him toward my car. "Get in."

He sat, defeated, in my passenger seat and all I could think about was finding Skye, then having my car detailed so it didn't smell like piss.

"I swear that I don't know where Skye is." His voice shook.

"You've already told me that. Give me something

more before I tear your head from your body," I seethed.

Right as he opened his mouth, my phone rang. I held my finger to stop him and fished my phone out.

"Donovan." My answer was clipped.

"Her car was abandoned about five miles north of her house."

"Find anything in her car?"

"Her purse and phone were sitting on the passenger seat."

"Fuck! I've got Harold. Have you heard from Hawke?"

"Not yet."

"Call him. I want the both of you to go back to the office and wait for my next instructions."

"You got it."

I ended the call and shoved it in my back pocket. "Speak, now," I commanded.

"I don't know where she is but I've got an idea. It will have to wait until later this evening. If we do something now, she will die."

I clenched my fist, wanting to end his miserable life. He trembled, covering his upper body with his arms. *Like that would keep him from my wrath.*

"You better not be fucking with me or so help me, even God will look the other way."

He placed his trembling hands in front of him in surrender. "I swear. You need me alive to help you."

I gritted my teeth, clenching my jaw so tight that the muscles screamed at me. My own pain was better than imagining what she was going through. All I wanted was to see her and make sure that she was alive. If I found out that Harold had anything to do with her kidnapping, I would make sure that he paid dearly.

"We are going to go to your office so you can change your fucking pants. I will be with you every step of the way. Do not even think about trying to skip out on me. Now get the fuck out of my car," I stated in a lethal voice.

This was either the smartest or the dumbest decision that I've ever made. Putting my trust in someone else's hands didn't make me feel comfortable at all. I placed a call to Brian and asked him for a huge favor. I was going to need the police force behind me, strictly to keep me on the right side of the law. I needed some kind of accountability in case I got trigger-happy. He was on board as backup if the need arose. He was going to let me handle things my way. I placed another call to Ryker. I told him and Hawke to be geared up and armed to the hilt. They were to be ready at a moment's notice. I knew that they would be. They loved Skye like a sister. They didn't show it but I knew my guys. Skye had weaseled her way into all of our hearts.

CHAPTER 32

I FELT LIKE DEATH WARMED OVER. My body ached all over. My shoulder pain had increased to the point that sleep was the only way that I could tolerate it. I lost precious time trying to figure out a way out but at this point I was too exhausted to care. I had to move and get my blood pumping properly through my limbs and sluggish mind. I gritted my teeth as I got to my knees. I held my bad arm to my side and wobbled to a standing position.

I walked in a bent position, looking for some kind of light to peek through a crack. I couldn't crawl and feel my way around; this was the best that I could do. I crept along the small room, scanning every crevice that I could. There was absolutely nothing. No window above and no other exit point. It was solid concrete and musty dirt. I spotted a water tank that looked as though it hooked into a well and a water heater. The only thing that I could think of was that I was trapped in some kind of basement. That meant that there was a possibility of a residence above me. *Was it the home of my abductor or was it abandoned?*

My foot snagged something solid and I tripped, coming down hard on the foreign object. I whimpered as the object dug into my shin. I moved off the object and picked it up. It was a scrap of a board. It was jagged on one end, as though it had been split from a two-by-four. I inched my way back toward the steel beam and stood the piece of wood up along the beam directly behind me. I was ready for whatever came next. It was too big to hide in my shirt and I couldn't get to it well with my hands tied. I would only have one or two good shots. I would have to make them count.

I sat in the darkness and thought of my parents, Jack, and Nash. Mainly Nash. Omar was but a blip of a picture. Nash took up the bulk of the images that played on my mind's screen. It was depressing that in what might be my last moments, I still dreamed of a man I wanted desperately but couldn't have. I kept replaying the scene from the last time I saw him. Curled up in his lap was the safest I had ever felt in my entire life. He was my home. I had wanted Omar to be that man for me. We had good chemistry. Shit, he made me laugh but he wasn't where my heart wanted to be.

I smiled at the thought of waking next to Nash and curled into his side every night. At this moment, even him bossing me around at work would be kind of fun. I would get to tease him every day, knowing that he would punish me sexually at night. He would be a hard man to be with. However, he had a soft side and I wanted to exploit that part of him. I didn't want protection. What I wanted was the way that he challenged me to be better. He would demand that I give him everything and I would.

I sat up straighter as the door opened again. I

went through the same routine every time the damn light flooded the dark room. I noticed that the black-clad figure had changed into a tennis-shoe, jean-wearing, fucking housewife. The way her eyes twinkled psychotically twisted my insides. The smile that pulled at her lips was one that made her features twist in to an ugly monster.

She stood at the foot of the stairs. "Surprise." Her voice hitched to an unbelievably high octave.

"Penny?" It was formed as a question.

I knew it was physically Penny but the shock of seeing her rendered me frozen. She was stronger than she portrayed. My body could attest to that.

She twirled. "In the flesh." Her smile grew wider.

"Why am I here? I am trying to help you." I tried to reason with her.

"Help me." Her laughter bubbled out like a hysterical cackle. "You aren't here to help me. Dear, you've broken up my family."

"How? All I was trying to do was find your daughter."

Her grin turned to a sneer. "All you've managed to do was dredge up long ago buried secrets." She sat on the bottom step and folded her hands in her lap as though she were trying to be patient with a toddler in trouble. "You know, the beatings stopped when Gray disappeared. When you started digging, he began to beat me all over again."

She stood quickly and paced the area in front of me. "You threw my affair back in Harold's face. I was finally able to become invisible again. I had a plan all worked out. I was going to finally leave him so that I could be with Brian. Gray's disappearance made that possible. Then you come in and start asking questions," she spat at me.

"What did you do with Gray?" I asked in a hushed voice.

"Why, nothing, dear. I don't know what happened to her. She was here when I left and gone when I came back. It was the best peace I've had in a long time."

"How can you be so cold? She was your daughter. She was all that you had."

She whipped around to face me. "She was what ruined everything. I was saddled with a child and the man I truly loved wanted nothing to do with me. The man I had married turned into a monster. I was trapped in this fucking house day and night. You couldn't possibly imagine what I've gone through."

No, I couldn't. If I had a child, I would've done anything and everything possible to keep them safe and loved. Above all else, loved.

"What is the point of all of this? What are you planning to do with me?"

Her smile came back brighter than the fluorescent bulb above the stairs. She stalked toward me. I scooted around the pole so that I was close to grabbing the board.

She squatted in front of me. "To make sure that you get everything that you deserve."

"That would be?"

"Pain, followed by death." She slapped me hard against the cheek. My head whipped to the side. I moved my jaw to ease the sting of her hand. I would not fight back yet. I had to keep her talking.

"Don't you want me to find Gray?"

She stood and stomped back and forth. "Didn't you hear a fucking word that I've said? No. I don't want you to find Gray. She was dead to me long before she went missing and I'm better for it," she shouted at me.

I cringed but not from the filth that she spouted. I moved my injured arm and grabbed the board, holding it protectively to my side. I twisted so that the board was still out of sight.

"How do you know that Gray is dead, if you don't know what happened to her?"

"I don't care either way. She is out of my hair and I get to do what I've always wanted."

"Don't you think that is kind of harsh? Why didn't you just divorce Harold and leave Gray with him?"

"For her to get what she's always wanted?" she asked, appalled.

"Wouldn't a shitty home life be better than the finality of death? You don't seem to care either way. Why would it have bothered you to just leave her?"

"You don't know my fucking life. All you do is poke around in other people's and destroy their lives," she screamed at me.

Call me a masochist, glutting for more punishment, but damn I enjoyed pissing her off. She was certifiable and I was driving this crazy train right to hell. I stood, holding on to the board, and squared off with her.

"I find the truth."

She rushed toward me, screaming that she was going to kill me. I planted my feet and with all of the strength that I had left, I swung the flat end of the board and hit her along her temple. The blow momentarily stunned her before she fell onto the ground. I turned the board over so that the sharpened end pointed down. I silently walked over to her and raised the board high above my head. I swung down, stopping just above her heart when I heard my name being called.

"Skye. Put the board down. She isn't worth it. Please, walk toward me. The authorities will deal with her."

His deep, masculine voice pulled at every fiber in my body. I followed his instructions and stepped over her still body. Once my foot hit the first step, I ran up them as fast as my body could until I felt his hard chest and the safety of his arms wrapping around me. He scooped me up and brought me the rest of the way out of the basement. A flood of uniformed police stormed the basement. They rolled her to her stomach and cuffed her. She had remained passed out the entire time that they had carried her out and into the ambulance. Once she was safely cuffed and out of sight, I relaxed.

"Ryker, Hawke, I want the two of you to follow that ambulance. Do not let her out of your sight until she is in a padded cell."

They took off without a word.

Nash guided me to a chair in the kitchen. He motioned for one of the officers to bring me a blanket. Omar stepped through the throng of officers, over to me, and wrapped a scratchy wool blanket around my shoulders. He bent and kissed my temple. It was a sweet gesture but not what I wanted at the moment. I wanted some space and a damn good explanation. I unapologetically ignored him.

I held my hands out in front of me and Nash sliced the plastic ties off my wrists. He used the pads of this thumbs to soothe the raw skin. I stared lovingly into his eyes. Everything that I wanted to say and felt shone through. Before I could say anything, I spotted a young woman out of the corner of my eye. Nash flashed his perfectly straight white teeth as recognition settled in.

"As soon as you hear what needs to be said, you are going to the hospital to get that shoulder checked out."

There was no room for an argument and I couldn't think of one anyway. My shoulder and ribs hurt like a bitch. First, I needed to see this through.

I twisted in my chair and stood, facing the young woman who I assumed was Gray.

I walked to her. "Gray?"

She nodded and burst into tears. I pulled her to me and hugged her like her mother should have. When her tears subsided and her body stopped trembling, I held her at arms length.

"Please tell me what is going on," I begged.

She turned toward her father with a small grin on her face. Even through it all, she was still grateful. "Daddy, I think that this is your story to tell."

I glanced over at Harold, not quite sure what to think.

"Penny was a very disturbed young woman. I didn't notice it until after she got pregnant."

I held up my hand. "Did you beat Penny? Do

you hate your daughter? Why did you say that you didn't have one?" I rushed out.

"Sit down, Skye, and let him tell you."

I didn't want to smile at Nash but I couldn't help it. He knew me so well.

"I've never laid a hand on my child or my wife. I have always loved Gray. She is the reason I did the things that I did. Anyway, when I met Penny she was fine, normal even. When she became pregnant with Gray, she became obsessed with things that were not real. She had made up this whole affair with Brian. She had never even met the man, only having seen him on TV. I didn't indulge her lying. I simply ignored her then. They had become more and more outlandish the further along her pregnancy went. After Gray was born, I had talked with the doctor and they had given her some medication. They diagnosed her with postpartum depression. When she took it, she seemed more like the woman I had married." He rubbed his hands down his face and sighed. "When she took it, she was a great mother. When she didn't, she became neglectful and was adamant that Gray was not her daughter."

"I'm pretty sure it was something more than postpartum," I interrupted him. That bitch was plumb crazy.

"I know. The medicine seemed to help so I didn't question it. After my business took off, I worked all the time. It was great to have my parents here to help with Gray. They watched her most of the time. When my mom got sick and they moved, Penny started acting different. It was as though she didn't have to pretend anymore now that no one was watching her. By that time, Gray was entering school and I could go to work with a clear conscience that Penny wouldn't inadvertently hurt her."

Gray came to stand by his side. She put a loving arm around her father. He looked up at her adoringly. "As Gray grew older, Penny would confide in her much like a friend. Gray became increasingly fearful of her mother. Penny wouldn't let her out of her sight and she accused Gray of trying to seduce me. I didn't know what to do. I couldn't control Penny's outbursts and I didn't know how to protect my daughter. So, I hid her. When I wasn't home and Penny went into one of her rages, I sent her to the only person that I could trust."

When he became quiet, I asked. "Who?"

"Glen Parker."

"I spoke with him and he made me believe that your relationship ended at the only job you did for him, except for playing cards at the country club."

"I spent a lot of my childhood with Mr. Glen. He had been a longtime friend of my daddy's. He took care of me. I moved in two years ago. I saw you the day that you came to speak with him. I stayed quiet because I didn't want to go back. I was petrified of my mother." Gray spoke with a maturity way beyond her years.

"When you were reported missing, why didn't you go to the police?"

She looked at me with a sympathetic face, as though I were the one with a shitty mother.

"What could they have done? My mother is crazy. She would inflict wounds on her body to make it look like my father beat her. That is what she told everyone and they believed her. She kept herself as meek as possible. Behind closed doors, she was a cold and calculating woman. The police would have been no different. I would've been taken away from him and kept in her care. Mr. Glen was our only hope. He had a niece who looked similar to me. I would go by her name instead of mine. It was easy to assimilate into her life. I continued school in a different district with her identity. Once I graduated I moved a state over, got a job that paid under the table and resumed my original name. When I visited, I came home to Mr. Glen's."

"I love my daughter. I've kept her out of the public eye so she would be forgettable. It may have been the wrong thing to do but it had kept her alive. I played the bastard to everyone around me, helping my wife's delusions become a reality. I knew that if she ever found out that Gray was still alive, she would've moved heaven and earth to make sure she no longer took a breath."

I blew out a puff of air and looked over to Brian. "What happens now? Can she post bail and be released? What was your involvement?"

He stood with his hands on his hips. "Harold had come to me some years back and told me that his wife was obsessed with me. He warned me to keep a close eye on my family. I've kept close tabs on her ever since. When Gray disappeared, I had personally taken an interest in the case. Like the detective, I could find nothing. Harold never alluded to anything. He played us all very well. I found nothing and let the whole thing go. I didn't stop watching Penny but she never showed any signs of being a danger to my family or me. As for bail, there will be none. She will be charged but I will make sure that she is locked up in a tightly secured mental facility. Everyone involved will be able to live their lives without fear."

I stood and went to hug Gray one more time. "I'm so thankful that you are safe," I whispered into her ear.

"I'm blessed to have had you searching for me. I am sorry for what my mother has done to you. She will get what she deserves."

I squeezed her hard one more time. "I'm ready to go, Nash."

He put his arm around my waist and helped me to his car. I eased into the leather seat and let him take the lead.

CHAPTER 33

THE BEAUTY OF BEING BANGED up was that I took a three-week paid vacation. Jack and I flew to Florida and spent our time on the beach. We took one day and went and talked to Diane. That was a hard and yet beautiful day. Diane was shocked and in disbelief when we told her about her sister. She cried tears of joy when I told her that Gray was alive and well. She still had her reservations about Harold but who could blame her with all the lies that she had been fed? In time, she would come to believe him much like I had after they had told me what had happened. Once it was confirmed by Gray herself, Diane would be on the next flight to Indiana to spend time with her niece.

With each passing day, my body healed. By the end of our stay, I had felt as good as new. Nash had been exceptionally positive about my taking an extended leave from work. What he didn't realize was that I would be back. Penny didn't break me; she did me one better—she made me stronger. She had opened my eyes wide and I looked at the world a little less naïvely. I kept in touch with Omar while I was gone. I had asked for some time and he had understood. I hadn't broken things off;

I simply needed to heal my mind and body.

Jack was my best supporter throughout this whole ordeal. She helped me get through the nightmares and made sure that I laughed, a lot. She never left my side. On a surprising note, Hawke had called her every night. She would excuse herself so that I couldn't hear her conversation. It pissed me off that I couldn't eavesdrop and she never told me a thing about it. We enjoyed our last week in sunny Florida. I hated to leave and yet I was ready to go home.

I pulled into my usual spot at the office. I walked up the flight of stairs with butterflies in my stomach. I hadn't seen Nash in twenty-one days, but who was counting. I stopped in front of his closed door and caught my breath. I looked over at Lisa. She smiled and nudged me through with her gentle mind-probing skills.

I wrapped my hand around the knob, twisted, and walked into my favorite place to be. I had missed the earthy smell of his cologne. It had engulfed me in a warm embrace the moment I stepped through the doorway. A grin lifted my mouth at the corners.

Nash sat at his desk with a sinister air around him. His facial features were twisted and contorted in concentration. He looked more dangerous than ever. My body hummed and moved slowly toward his silent call. He lifted his head and his stormy eyes took me in from head to toe and back up.

"Miss me?"

"Skye." Surprise filled his voice.

"In the flesh." I bounced on my toes with my hands clasped in front of me.

He swiveled his chair to the side and stood. I rounded the desk and stopped inches from him. He yanked me to his chest and wrapped his massive arms around my body. I hugged him back, needing to feel a connection with him. I hadn't talked to him the whole time I was gone. I hadn't realized how much I had missed him until I was engulfed in his masculinity.

His lips lingered along my hairline. They never ventured any further. My disappointment was loud and clear. His chuckle reverberated along my spine, sending a fresh wave of heated goose bumps to bead along my skin. He yanked me away from his body and held me at arm's length. I didn't have the courage to look at him.

He took his index finger and lifted my chin. Once I looked into the depths of his gray eyes, I was lost. He leaned his head down and placed his full lips over mine. It was a sensual kiss of lost lovers who had found each other again. It wasn't full of promises or good-byes. It was filled with yearning, desire, and the unknown.

OTHER BOOKS

ACKNOWLEDGMENTS

Thank you to all of my family and friends who continuously encourage me to do what I love. A huge thank-you to all of my beta readers: my mom, Kim H., Melissa L., Norma S., Jamie M., and Erin F., and Jenn M. A special thank-you to Kim H., for pushing me to produce books for her to read, and to Melissa L. for providing a ton of ideas. This book wouldn't be as entertaining without all of your input. Thank you to my editor, Faith Williams, for making this book a smoother read. Thank you to the Killion Group for formatting, designing the cover, and helping to publish it properly.

I'd like to thank all of my readers for taking the time to read, send me feedback, and post reviews. Without you, they are just words on a page. Thank you very much for being an essential part of my journey.

ABOUT THE AUTHOR

Jenni Bradley lives in Florida, with her husband, three daughters, three dogs, one cat, and four horses: pretty much a small, funny farm where there is never a dull day. She enjoys riding most days. The other days are usually met with hard dirt and a happy horse.

You can find Jenni online at *www.jennibradley. com* to find out more, plus news on upcoming books.

You can also find Jenni on Facebook at www. facebook.com/JenniBradley-1453178658324928/

Goodreads at www.goodreads.com/author/show/14237910.Jenni_Bradley